GRUMPY COZY CHRISTMAS

MEREDITH SUMMERS

CHAPTER 1

Ginger sighed happily as she fluffed a pillow on the antique four-poster bed, taking in the cozy room with its sloped ceilings, floral wallpaper, and crackling fireplace. Her suitcase lay open on the floor, spilling clothes onto the colorful oriental rug. As she gazed out the frost-lined window at the blanket of snow covering the ground and trees, a sense of peace settled over her.

This holiday trip to Pinecone Falls, Vermont, was exactly what she needed after the stuffiness of the city, and the Cozy Holly Inn was the perfect place to stay while she was here.

A soft knock interrupted her reverie. "Ms. Sanders, did you need anything?" Ida, the innkeeper at the quaint old Victorian inn, poked her head into the room.

Ginger smiled, warmth flooding her at the woman's thoughtfulness. "No, thank you. Everything is perfect."

Ginger finished hanging her clothes in the antique armoire and zipped the suitcase shut. As she stood there, lost in thought, her phone buzzed on the wooden nightstand.

It was a text from Mason. *Be there in 20 minutes!*

Mason was not just a friend to Ginger; he was like a brother. They had grown up next door to each other and had been inseparable since they were in kindergarten. As her own family had never quite captured the essence of a warm Christmas holiday, preferring to spend the holidays in tropical islands, Mason had extended an invitation to spend Christmas in the quaint town of Pinecone Falls.

She was excited to see him. Yet, as she tucked her phone into her pocket, she felt a tiny bit nervous at the prospect of meeting his new girlfriend, Kristen, for the first time. They'd only been dating a short time, but she could tell that Mason had already fallen hard. She was happy for him and really wanted to like Kristen, but more than that, she wanted Kristen to like *her*.

"I'm sure we'll get along fine," she said to herself as

she took one last longing glance at the snow-laden landscape outside the window. She still had twenty minutes to explore the charming inn that was to be her home for the holiday. Having only caught a fleeting impression of the place while checking in, she was eager to take a closer look.

As Ginger stepped out of her room and wandered down the creaky staircase, she marveled at how the Cozy Holly Inn seemed to have stepped directly off the pages of a Christmas movie. The Victorian house brimmed with charm and warmth, and it was decorated to the hilt with garland, twinkle lights, and holiday décor. The scents of fresh pine boughs and cookies filled the air.

As she descended, her fingertips trailed along the pine garland. It was a white pine, which was unusual. Typically, one used balsam firs. She studied the needles closely, her scientist brain calculating the health of the tree. The needles were a little dry but otherwise good. Her brain forgot to pay attention to what her feet were doing as she started to automatically calculate the perfect fertilizer for the tree and...

"Oof!" Ginger stumbled as she reached the last step of the staircase, her foot getting caught in a rug at the foot of the stairs. She caught herself just in time with a theatrical spin before straightening up and patting down her disheveled hair in an attempt to regain some composure.

"Dear me!" exclaimed Ida, bustling forward from behind the check-in desk. "Are you all right, my dear?" A warm smile crossed Ida's plump, rosy cheeks as she steadied Ginger, her eyes twinkling like stars.

"Yes. No worries," Ginger assured the woman. "Happens all the time."

The downside of having an ever-active mind was that she rarely looked where she was going and often bumbled around like a clumsy oaf. Her thoughts tended to run away with her, distracting her from her physical surroundings.

"Your decorations are lovely." Ginger gestured vaguely at the garlands draped along the banister, hoping to draw attention away from her clumsiness.

"Ah, yes! Christmas is such a magical time, isn't it?" Ida beamed, clasping her hands together. "I simply love transforming the inn into a festive wonderland! Speaking of which, would you care for some freshly baked cookies and hot chocolate? It's a tradition around here, and we always have some on hand."

Ginger's stomach gave an appreciative growl at the mention of cookies, and she gratefully accepted Ida's offer. The innkeeper bustled into the kitchen and returned to thrust a steaming mug of hot chocolate topped with whipped cream into her hands. She also had a plate piled high with cookies shaped like snowflakes and reindeer.

"Thank you," Ginger murmured then sipped the rich, velvety cocoa, feeling the warmth spread through her body like a cozy blanket.

"Anytime, dear!" Ida replied, giving Ginger a wink. "Now, why don't you make yourself at home in the living room? There's a lovely group of people knitting by the fireplace. I'm sure they'd love some company."

Knitting? Ginger mused as she wandered toward the living room, cookie crumbs tumbling onto her scarf like snowflakes. She had recently taken up the craft herself, although her skills left much to be desired. Still, it was a pleasant way to pass the time and keep her hands occupied when her thoughts threatened to spiral.

"Hello there!" called an elderly woman from the cluster of knitters, her needles clicking together like festive castanets. "I'm Myrtle. Would you care to join us?"

"Actually," Ginger said hesitantly, "I've recently started knitting myself. I'm not very good, but... well, practice makes perfect, right?"

"Absolutely!" The woman laughed, patting the

cushion beside her. "Come, sit with us! We'd be delighted to share our tips and expertise with you."

"And we have extra yarn and needles." Another woman gestured toward a large tote bag. Needles of all sizes were sticking out of the top, along with colorful skeins of yarn and something else. It was fluffy and white... and moving!

Suddenly, a ball of yarn flew out of the tote. A white cat followed it, batting at the yarn and then jumping on the unraveling strands. Everyone laughed.

"That's Kringle, the Cozy Holly Inn resident cat," Myrtle said.

"Hello there, Kringle." Ginger bent down to scratch behind the cat's ears. It purred contentedly, its large blue eyes blinking up at her slowly as if to say, "Welcome to the Cozy Holly Inn."

"Kringle is our unofficial mascot," Mabel explained with a chuckle. "He brings an extra layer of coziness to the place, don't you think?"

"Absolutely," Ginger agreed, smiling down at the cat as he scurried off after the ball of yarn again. She felt a small pang in her heart. She'd always wanted a cat, but her family hadn't been keen on pets, and she couldn't have one in her condo.

"Pick up some needles and join us," said a woman in her early sixties, her needles still flying as she looked up over the rim of her tortoise reading glasses at Ginger.

"I'd love to, but I'm waiting for my friend." Ginger glanced out the window to see Mason coming up the front steps. He was with a woman with long, wavy chestnut hair. Their cheeks were red with cold, and their eyes were bright as they stole glances at each other. "And there he is. Nice meeting you all."

"We meet here every day during the holiday season. You simply must join us!" Myrtle called out as Ginger went to meet Mason at the front door. Ginger couldn't help but feel her heart swell with warmth. This was exactly what she wanted for the holidays. Well, this and to fix the problem with the trees at the Woodward family's tree farm.

Mason had invited her for two reasons. One was to spend the holidays together. Mason was like a brother, and his dad, Kent, was like a father. The other reason was that Kristen's family tree farm had an issue with their Christmas trees. Ginger was the perfect person to take on the task, and once she took on a task, she never failed. Of course there was the little problem that Christmas was only two weeks away. If she wanted to get those trees healthy again, she'd have to work fast.

CHAPTER 2

"Ah, young love," Ida mused, her eyes twinkling with amusement. "Don't worry, dear. Your time will come."

Ginger stifled a laugh at the thought of herself being swept off her feet by some dashing stranger. In reality, the most excitement she'd had lately was the prospect of attending a knitting club meeting. Shaking off her thoughts, she stepped outside to greet her friends.

"Hey, Ginger!" Mason called out, his warm grin reaching his eyes.

"Good to see you, buddy." She hugged him tightly and gave him a sisterly kiss on the cheek. "And you must be Kristen." She turned to face the woman standing beside Mason, who smiled warmly.

"Nice to finally meet you, Ginger," Kristen said, her blue eyes sparkling with sincerity. "Mason has told me so much about you."

"Hopefully all good things," Ginger joked, feeling her nerves dissipate as the three of them exchanged pleasantries. After all, if Kristen could make her beloved friend this happy, she had to be a good person, right?

"Of course!" Kristen reassured her. "I can't wait for you to join us at the farm. I have a feeling we're going to get along just great."

"Me too," Ginger agreed, trying to ignore the slight pang of envy that bubbled up at seeing the two of them so happy together. What was up with that? Ginger had never been the type to need a man or pine for a relationship. Still... it might be nice to have a special someone to share things with. But since no special someone was on the horizon, she would be completely content by herself.

"Speaking of the farm," Ginger began, her eyes lighting up with excitement as she tapped into her inner botanist, "I've been thinking about your trees. I've come up with a formula that might help improve their health and overall growth."

"Really?" Kristen appeared pleasantly surprised. "That's so thoughtful of you. We could definitely use some expert advice." She hesitated for a moment before adding, "But there's one thing you should know..."

Ginger leaned in, curious to hear what sort of insider information her new friend had to share.

"Whatever you do," Kristen warned, her voice dropping to a conspiratorial whisper, "be careful about mentioning your ideas for the trees to my brother, Ethan, if you happen to run into him at the farm. He's, well, a bit sensitive when it comes to our trees."

"Sensitive? How so?"

Kristen sighed, a fond smile playing on her lips. "He's just very protective of the farm, especially since our dad passed away. He takes pride in his work and wants to do everything himself. Just trust me on this one. Tread lightly when you talk to him. You probably won't see him anyway. He's pretty reclusive."

"He's a good guy, though, once you get to know him. He's had some tragedies, so he's quiet," Mason said.

"And a bit grumpy," Kristen added. Then her face softened. "Of course it's hard to blame him, given that his wife passed in a car accident. That's when he withdrew. He used to be really outgoing."

Ginger's heart went out to Ethan even though she'd never met him. "A car accident? That's terrible."

Kristen nodded. "It was five years ago. He seems to be making peace with it now."

"All right," Ginger agreed, intrigued by the image of a wounded, brooding tree farmer lurking among the pines. "Your secret is safe with me. But if he asks why I'm wandering around the farm with test tubes and soil samples, I can't make any promises."

"Fair enough." Kristen laughed, shaking her head at Ginger's playful exaggeration. "Let's just hope he's too busy wrestling with a stubborn tree trunk or something to notice."

"What do you guys say? Should we go check the trees out?" Mason asked, motioning toward the door.

"Let's go," Ginger agreed. She was eager to inspect the trees and get her brain working on the exact formula that would restore them to health even if it did mean avoiding the reclusive tree farmer.

CHAPTER 3

Ethan Woodward didn't visit Sarah's grave as much as he used to. That was a good thing, right? He hoped so. But he still made a trip there at least once a week. He made sure flowers were planted in summer and brushed the snow off the top of the grave in winter. At first, of course, the visits had been gut-wrenching, but now they were peaceful. And he was never alone. A bright-red cardinal seemed to always be sitting in the pine tree, watching him. Its cheerful chirps lifted his spirits. He imagined that somehow Sarah's spirit was in the bird, letting him know she was with him. But that was silly.

He'd been at the cemetery when his phone beeped with an email from Mayor Thompson. Cemetery time was sacred time, though, and he wasn't going to soil it by reading an email from the mayor, so he'd put the phone in his pocket.

But now he was back at the tree farm, trudging through the snow between the rows of balsam pines, their brown needles drooping sadly toward the cold ground. His boots crunched on the icy path as he remembered to check his phone. He stared at the ominous email from Mayor Thompson glaring up at him from the screen. With a heavy sigh that billowed out in a cloud of resigned frustration, Ethan pocketed the phone and rested his head against the rough bark of the tree beside him. Somewhere on this huge tree farm, there had to be at least one tree that wasn't inundated with brown needles.

Ethan's gaze shifted from the sickly tree to the sky above, as if willing the heavens to provide some divine intervention. He knew he couldn't blame the balsam pines for their sad state; after all, it was his responsibility to see them through this tough time. But with the mayor's email fresh in his mind, he couldn't help but feel the pressure mounting.

"Dear Mr. Woodward," the email had read, "I trust that you have selected a suitable tree for the upcoming tree-lighting ceremony. As you know, this event is of great importance to our town, and I would like to personally inspect your choice before giving my approval..." The words seemed to echo ominously in Ethan's head.

Laughter shattered the quiet despair that enveloped him. Looking up, he spotted his sister and her new boyfriend standing by a tree, holding hands, and sharing a laugh. How could they find amusement at a time like this?

"Nothing funny about trees dying," Ethan muttered to himself as he strode toward the couple, his brow furrowed with concern.

The cold air nipped at his face as he approached Kristen and Mason, both bundled up in their winter gear. Despite the weight of his worries, he couldn't help but feel a warmth in his chest as he watched them. They looked happy together, and he was glad for his sister. Just because he would never be happy again like that didn't mean he didn't want that for Kristen.

"Hey, sis," Ethan called out, forcing a smile onto his face. "Mason."

"Hey, Ethan!" Kristen beamed back at him, her cheeks rosy from the cold.

Mason raised a hand in greeting.

"What's so funny?" Ethan asked, trying to keep the edge from his voice. "These trees need more nit..." His words trailed off as he noticed something peculiar: a pair of blue-jean-clad legs sticking out from under the very tree Kristen and Mason were standing in front of.

"Um... is there a reason there's someone under that tree?" Ethan ventured cautiously, doing his best not to stare at the shapely derrière attached to the legs, which were half hidden by the low branches.

Just as he was about to inquire further, the tree rustled, and out popped a woman. She was covered in sap and pine needles. Her fiery-red hair was a chaotic mess, but her smile was bright, and she still managed to look adorable in an endearingly disheveled sort of way.

"Ethan, allow me to introduce Ginger Sanders, my childhood friend," Mason said with a chuckle. "Ginger's family usually spends holidays in the tropics, but she's always wanted to experience a snowy Christmas, so I invited her out here."

"Nice to meet you, Ginger," Ethan said, immediately reverting to grump mode as he extended his hand cautiously.

Ginger clasped it in a viselike grip. Her hand was cold and sticky.

Ethan tried to suppress a grimace as he felt the sticky sap rub off on his palm. He glanced down at his hand, now covered with goo, and then back up at Ginger, who looked just as mortified as he felt.

"I'm so sorry," she said, wiping her hand on her coat. "I was just trying to prop up this branch so I could get a closer look at the trunk. I didn't mean to get sap all over you."

Ethan waved it off with a forced smile, his eyes still fixed on the gooey residue clinging to his skin. "No problem, happens all the time."

Ginger somehow managed to grimace apologetically and beam her high-wattage smile at the same time.

"So what were you doing under the tree?" Ethan glanced at Kristen and Mason. He remembered Mason mentioning that he worked with someone who was some sort of plant expert, but Ethan had been picturing a balding forty-five-year-old with a pocket protector, not a beautiful woman.

"Oh. Well..." Ginger looked at Mason and Kristen uncertainly. "I have a way with trees, and Kristen mentioned yours need a little help. Just thought I might take a peek and see if I could suggest something."

"Ginger's being modest," Mason said. "She's one of the world's leading agricultural scientists."

"I appreciate you taking a look, but I don't think there's anything you can do. I've already tried amending the soil and changing the pH. It's more difficult in winter, when the ground is frozen, of course." Ethan hoped that was enough to discourage her. The last thing he needed was this chirpy ray of sunshine tagging along and distracting him from the job of making the trees healthy. He didn't have time to babysit someone.

"She might have some ideas that you didn't consider," Kristen said softly.

Ethan could see the determination in Kristen's eyes, and he couldn't fault her for it. After all, she was deeply invested in the tree farm as well and genuinely wanted to help. However, deep down, he knew that the responsibility of fixing the problem ultimately fell on his shoulders.

Ethan's phone pinged. Probably another message from the mayor. He glanced at Ginger. Her face was covered in sap and pine needles, but her eyes were bright, as if she was excited about a solution. Maybe it wouldn't hurt to hear her out.

Ethan hesitated, his eyes flicking between Ginger and the trees. He didn't want to admit that he needed help, but Ethan knew he was running out of options. With a sigh, he finally nodded. "Fine, you can take a look at the trees later. But I can't promise anything will come of it."

Though Ethan desperately wanted the trees

healthy, he doubted Ginger could do anything, and he hoped this was the last he'd see of Little Miss Sunshine. What did an agricultural scientist know about pine trees, anyway? She worked with all kinds of plants; he specialized in one type—evergreens. And he had enough problems with the mayor and the balsam firs that he didn't have time to deal with another one. The best solution would be to act his grumpiest, not encourage her to spend any more time here than necessary, and hopefully, she would soon go away and let him tend to his problems in peace.

❄

GINGER STUDIED ETHAN'S FACE, taking in the lines of worry and the weariness that seemed to weigh down his shoulders. She couldn't help but notice his handsome features too—his tall frame, dark hair, and captivating eyes.

She could see how much this problem was bothering him, and she couldn't help but feel a surge of sympathy. It was clear he was reluctant to accept help, but she knew he needed it. And she was not one to back down from a challenge. That was how she'd gotten to be the best in her field.

"I've done some research, and I'm putting together a formula that may help," Ginger said.

Ethan hesitated, his eyes flicking to the message on his phone. He sighed, rubbing the back of his neck. "All right. Tell me about it."

Ginger's spirits rose, but she kept her tone casual. "Well, I noticed some signs of a nutrient deficiency in the needles. I'd like to take some samples and run some tests. It's a long shot, but it might give us a better idea of what's going on."

Ethan furrowed his brow, clearly considering her suggestion. "I don't know. I've tried so many things already. What makes you think this will work?"

"I've had success with a similar problem before. I can't guarantee anything, but it's worth a try," Ginger said, her enthusiasm undeterred by Ethan's guarded demeanor. "If I could get the needle samples, I might be able to find out more."

Ethan's gaze flicked from Ginger to the trees to his sister. "Okay, I guess that can't hurt."

Ginger smiled, appreciating the small victory. "Great. I'll come back later to gather the samples and run some tests. Hopefully we can figure this out quickly."

Ginger felt a flutter of excitement. She loved the challenge of figuring out what a plant needed to be restored to health, but her excitement was more than that. She liked the Woodward family. Even though Ethan did seem a bit grumpy, she sensed a vulnerability lurking underneath the rough exterior. And Kristen was very sweet. Ginger could see how worried they both were, which made her even more determined to fix their problem. Maybe with a bit of hard work and some luck, she could pull off a Christmas miracle for the Woodward family.

CHAPTER 4

As Ethan walked back to his cabin, the snow crunched beneath his boots and the cold air nipped at his cheeks. The tree farm was blanketed in a layer of white, transforming the landscape into a serene winter wonderland. The snow-dusted boughs of the trees glistened in the soft light, lending an ethereal quality to the scene.

Just then, George, his mother's cat, skittered out from behind a tree, surprising Ethan. He had been reluctant to bond with the feline, but there was something comforting about the animal's presence. Ethan decided to unburden himself in a one-sided conversation with George.

"Hey, George," Ethan said, crouching to scratch the

cat's ears. "You wouldn't believe what happened today."

George meowed and rubbed against Ethan's legs. The cat's sable-and-tan facial markings were glossy and shiny against the white fur of his chest. He looked up, blinking his brilliant blue eyes as if encouraging Ethan to continue.

"I met this woman, Ginger. She's a friend of Mason's and some sort of tree expert. She thinks she can help with our tree problem, but I'm not so sure," Ethan confessed, glancing around at the snow-covered trees surrounding them.

George tilted his head, as if he were genuinely considering Ethan's concerns.

"You should have seen her, George. She was a mess, covered in sap and pine needles, but somehow still... beautiful. And those eyes, so full of hope and determination." Ethan sighed, feeling a strange mix of frustration and admiration for the redhead.

George meowed in response, as if offering some sage advice.

"Yeah, I know. I should probably give her a chance," Ethan admitted, standing up and brushing snow off his knees. "But it's just so hard to let someone else in on this, especially when I'm not sure if she can really help."

With a soft purr, George followed Ethan as they continued toward the cabin. The snowflakes drifted gently to the ground, blanketing the tree farm in a quiet hush. The peaceful atmosphere belied the turmoil Ethan felt inside.

CHAPTER 5

Ginger rushed into the Cozy Holly Inn, ignoring the welcoming warmth and scent of cinnamon and nutmeg as she pulled a handful of pine needles out of her pocket. She hurried up the stairs to her room, trying not to let her excitement bubble over—or to trip on her own feet. She imagined herself a cute, perky, and determined heroine in one of those heartwarming Christmas movies, ready to save the day while maintaining her quirky charm. In reality, she probably looked more like a flustered academic who'd just discovered a new treatment for plants.

Once inside her room, she carefully laid out the pine needles on the desk and began setting up her portable testing kit. Her fingers fumbled with the tiny vials and droppers, but she managed to keep her clumsy nature at bay. At least, for now.

"Okay, Ginger, you can do this," she whispered to herself, peering through the microscope at the delicate needles, searching for clues hidden within their green depths. "No pressure, just the future of an entire family business resting on your shoulders."

She prepared slides, mixed solutions, and scribbled notes furiously, determination fueling her every move. As she analyzed each sample, she couldn't help but picture Ethan's face, his guarded expression melting away slowly like snowflakes on a warm windowsill when she finally brought him good news.

"Snap out of it, Ginger," she scolded herself, shaking her head. "Focus on the needles, not the grumpy guy who can't decide whether to trust you or not."

With a renewed sense of purpose, Ginger dove back into her work, her brain buzzing with theories and potential solutions. Once, she had to rush back to her rental car for more vials, and Kringle followed her back to the room, where he took up residence on the windowsill like a furry supervisor. She smiled at him, feeling a strange connection with the curious creature.

"All right, Kringle, let's save some trees, shall we?" Ginger glanced up from her microscope and found

Kringle staring at her, his sky-blue eyes shimmering with curiosity. She chuckled. "You know, Kringle, you remind me of the kids back in my old lab," she said, carefully adjusting a few pine needles on the glass slide. "Always peeking over my shoulder, trying to figure out what I was up to."

The cat simply blinked, as if acknowledging her comparison. Ginger continued, "It's nice to have a little company, though." She sighed, peering through the microscope again. "I've been feeling a bit lonely lately, but this problem is a great distraction."

Kringle seemed to nod in understanding, shifting his position on the windowsill to get a better view of her work.

Just then, there was a soft knock on the door. Ginger jumped, startled by the intrusion into her one-sided conversation with Kringle. She composed herself quickly, calling out, "Come in!"

The door creaked open, and Ida peered in, a concerned expression on her face. "I noticed you've been working away in here for quite a while, dear," she said kindly. "I thought you might be hungry."

Ginger was about to protest that she wasn't hungry at all when her stomach gave a loud rumble, betraying her. "Oh, well, now that you mention it..." she mumbled, rubbing her stomach sheepishly.

"Never fear, I whipped up something special for you," Ida declared, revealing a plate containing a generous sandwich of turkey, stuffing, and cranberry sauce.

"Wow, that looks amazing," Ginger marveled, accepting the offering with grateful eyes as her mouth watered at the sight of the delicious sandwich.

"Nothing like a homemade meal to keep you going." Ida winked, her smile warm and motherly as she handed Ginger a glass of milk.

"Thank you so much, Ida. You're too kind." Ginger was overwhelmed by the innkeeper's thoughtfulness. She couldn't remember the last time someone had cared enough to bring her a meal while she was working. At the company, they just kept piling work on. The faster she was, the more work they gave her and never once a free lunch. She was starting to feel like she wasn't appreciated at work, but had only just barely started looking around for other jobs. Another reason for this extended vacation was to clear her head about work and figure out what she really wanted to do.

"Think nothing of it, dear." Ida waved her hand dismissively, then her gaze skirted over Ginger's shoulder. "What in the world are you doing in here, anyway?"

"Um, well, it's... a work project," Ginger replied

hesitantly. She hated being evasive with Ida, but she wanted to respect the Woodward family's privacy. "Don't worry. I'm not going to blow up the inn or anything."

Ida chuckled, clearly amused by Ginger's response. "I'm not worried, dear. Whatever it is, I'm sure you're doing great work. Enjoy your sandwich!"

"Thanks for bringing it." Ginger took a bite of the sandwich. The savory flavors of turkey and stuffing mingled with the sweet cranberry sauce danced on her tongue. She closed her eyes in delight. "Mmm! This is heavenly!"

"I do my best," Ida said.

"Thank you again, Ida. You're a lifesaver," Ginger mumbled around a mouthful of food as the door closed behind the innkeeper.

"Okay, Kringle, back to business." Taking another hearty bite of her sandwich, Ginger suddenly noticed a drop of cranberry sauce escape from the bread and land squarely on her pristine white cashmere sweater. "Oh, not again!" she groaned, staring down at the blob of red amid the white. This wasn't the first sweater she'd ruined, but this one was a favorite. *Time to buy a new one.*

She blotted up the blob, stripped the soiled sweater off, and threw it on her bed, then she rummaged in the closet for a stain-free one. This one was red.

Ginger managed to finish her sandwich without dripping on the red sweater. Then she returned to analyzing her samples. After another hour, she looked up at the cat, her eyes sparkling with excitement as she scribbled down the last of her calculations. "I think we've got it!"

The cat, clearly uninterested in her scientific breakthrough, had moved to the bed. He yawned and stretched languidly.

Ginger called Mason to fill him in.

"Hey, Ginger," Mason answered, his voice warm and friendly. "How's my favorite tree whisperer doing?"

Ginger laughed. "I think I may have actually found a potential formula that could help the trees on the Woodward farm."

"Really?" he exclaimed, genuine excitement in his voice. "That's amazing!"

"Yeah, I need to look at one more thing, but I was wondering if I do come up with a formula, would we actually be able to apply it to the trees? Ethan didn't exactly seem like he was totally on board."

"Ah," Mason replied, understanding her dilemma. "Ethan can be a tough nut to crack, can't he? But the

Woodwards need something. You just come up with the formula and leave Ethan to me, Kristen, and Dorothy."

"Will do," Ginger replied then hung up the phone with a renewed sense of purpose.

As she looked down at Kringle, who was now using her stained sweater as a makeshift bed, she couldn't help but smile. At least the sweater wouldn't go to waste.

CHAPTER 6

The scent of freshly baked cookies filled the cozy kitchen at the Woodward farmhouse. Dorothy, Mason, Kristen, and Kent were gathered around the well-worn wooden table.

Everyone was looking at Mason, who had just hung up from a call with Ginger. Dorothy reached over to the plate of cookies and took an iced snowman. The sugar cookies were her favorite part about the holidays, and she always had a supply on hand. She and Kristen had stayed up late into the night baking this batch. She loved that her daughter was home to stay now and that they could do things together like that.

"So what did she say?" Kristen asked.

Mason smiled. Dorothy liked Mason. He was a

nice guy and handsome too, with gray eyes and lightly stubbled jaw. She hoped his romance with Kristen would last. He'd make a great son-in-law, and she liked Kent enough to be family too.

"She might be onto a formula that could work on the trees," Mason said.

"Really?" Kristen's eyes widened with hope as she brushed an auburn curl behind her ear.

Mason nodded. "She said something about how she studied the needles to figure out what nutrients they were missing then doing some calculations to figure out what elements would get those nutrients into the tree fast. Honestly, she's such a brainiac that I really never understand exactly what she's talking about."

Dorothy wasn't sure she liked the sound of that. If they didn't understand what Ginger was doing, maybe it was a mistake to let her apply the formula to the trees. Dorothy knew the farm was in trouble, but she was worried about making things worse. The farm had been in the family for generations, and the death of her husband had put her in charge. It was up to her to make sure it remained viable for future generations. Perhaps the only one who felt that responsibility more heavily was her son, Ethan.

"I'd like to meet Ginger," Dorothy said. "I'm not entirely sure we should try something now."

"You'll like her, Mom." Kristen petted George, who was curled in her lap. He let out a soft purr, his ear flicking slightly.

"You can trust her, Dot," Kent said. "I've known her since she was a little tyke, and that girl is a genius when it comes to plants. If she says that this formula has potential, then we should definitely give it a shot."

"Besides, Mom," Kristen added, animatedly waving a half-eaten cookie, crumbs falling onto her lap, "we don't have much to lose by trying it out, do we?"

Dorothy trusted Kent and Kristen. Taking a slow, thoughtful sip from her steaming teacup, she nodded. "True. I guess it probably can't hurt. Good luck getting your brother on board, though. You know how stubborn he is."

"Stubborn? Who's stubborn?" Ethan's deep voice rang out from the back mudroom, as if on cue. The group fell silent as he sauntered into the warm, inviting kitchen and leaned against the doorframe, his arms crossed over his broad chest.

The room seemed to hold its breath. Even George stopped purring and jumped out of Kristen's lap.

"Cookie, dear?" Dorothy slid the plate across the

table, and Ethan detached himself from the doorway and grabbed a reindeer cookie with a small red heart candy for a nose and two tiny chocolate chips for eyes.

"So I heard you met Mason's friend Ginger earlier." Dorothy figured that might be a good way to cautiously broach the subject with her son.

Ethan's expression collapsed into its usual scowl, but Dorothy thought she saw a spark of interest in his dark eyes.

Kent cleared his throat nervously, while Kristen tried to hide her grin behind her cookie.

"Yeah, she was rolling around under the trees. Kind of odd, if you ask me." Ethan ignored George, who was doing figure eights around his ankles.

Dorothy knew Ethan pretended to be immune to the cat's charms, but she'd seen him petting the cat and talking to him when he thought no one was looking.

"She was checking out the health of the balsams. She's trying to help with our problem," Kristen said.

"Uh huh." Ethan nodded.

"She thinks she has a solution," Mason added.

"She does?" Ethan shoved the last of his cookie into his mouth.

"She's pretty smart," Kent chimed in.

"Did she test her solution? What tree farm? How

long did it take the trees to recover?" Ethan asked.

They all looked at each other. "Umm, I think it's specific to our trees," Kristen said.

"So it's risky," Ethan grumbled.

"Maybe so, dear, but we do have a pressing issue. Unless you're coming here to tell us that you've solved the problem?"

Dorothy felt a pang of guilt at the way her son's expression darkened even further. She hadn't meant that as a jab. She was actually hoping he *had* solved the problem. People were starting to show up at the tree lot, asking for balsams. So far John, who worked the lot, had been able to persuade them that blue spruces were much better, but that wasn't going to last forever. Besides, the mayor wanted the tallest balsam for the tree lighting, just like her husband had donated for the past thirty years.

Ethan sighed and grumbled, "I'm trying a few things."

Dorothy hated to see Ethan in such a state of perpetual grouchiness. He hadn't always been that way. He'd once been happy and carefree. But the accident that had taken his wife from him had also taken his happiness. Dorothy could understand, but she also knew he was young enough to be able to move on and grab some happiness. Judging by that little spark she'd seen when she mentioned Ginger's name, Ethan might finally be open to that. If she played her cards right, maybe she could push things so that little spark would have a chance to ignite a flame of happiness inside him again—if only he let it.

"It might not be a bad idea to try more things. Ginger is an expert and pretty smart, from what Kent says," Dorothy said.

Kristen nodded her approval. "I say we add Ginger's solution to the things we are trying. What have we got to lose?"

CHAPTER 7

What have we got to lose? Only the entire tree farm, Ethan thought as he trudged through the snow back toward his cabin. But his sister was right—he was running out of ideas, and right now, he couldn't afford to be picky.

What if her concoctions ruin all the trees?

On the flip side, what if they didn't? The alternative was equally frightening. If he decided not to let her use her serums—or whatever she called them—and the tree farm withered and died under his watch, he would carry the weight of that guilt. And it would be all his fault because his mother and Kristen had wanted to give Ginger a try.

As he crossed the yard, the snow crunched beneath his feet in an almost musical rhythm, and the crisp winter air tickled his nose as he took a deep breath. He tugged on his hat and scarf—both were knitted by his mother in a comically loud pattern that could only have been described as "festive"—and headed toward the woods.

The small house he lived in—a log cabin built by his grandfather—sat about a quarter mile away down a dirt road. It was just the right distance to be close to his family but far enough to be isolated when he wanted to be, which was most of the time.

He had a four-wheel-drive truck, but he enjoyed walking through the woods, looking at the trees and birds. He'd always been drawn to nature, and the solitude of the woods in winter was appealing.

A familiar furry figure emerged from the trees, bounding through the snow. With a graceful leap, he landed in one of Ethan's footprints before hopping to the next, providing a comical sight that was impossible not to smile at.

"George!" Ethan chuckled, momentarily forgetting his troubles. "You always know how to make an entrance, don't you? You'd better get back home. My mother will be mad."

The cat simply stared back at him, his blue eyes glinting with mischief.

"All right, fine. You can come along," Ethan

relented, his voice softening. “But don’t tell anyone I let you, got it?”

George mewed nonchalantly, clearly unfazed by the notion of being a rule breaker.

As they continued through the woods, Ethan found himself opening up to his unlikely confidant. “You know, George, sometimes I just feel like I’m carrying the weight of the entire farm on my shoulders,” he admitted, pausing to lean against a tree trunk and look down at the cat.

George didn’t offer any advice. He usually didn’t, but Ethan liked discussing his problems with George. He didn’t really have anyone else to talk to. He didn’t want to bother his mother or sister, and talking things out with George was better than just talking to himself. Of course, Ethan didn’t want to let anyone know he confided in the cat, so when his family was around, he pretended to be indifferent. Ethan didn’t want anyone to see his soft side, because that was how you opened yourself up to getting hurt.

Ethan pushed off the tree and continued on with George following behind him, playfully hopping from footprint to footprint.

“I am getting quite worried about the trees. The blue spruces are fine, but people love balsams, and if word gets out that our balsams aren’t any good, people will get their trees somewhere else, even the spruces." He paused, and George tilted his head, as though listening intently to every word. "I've tried all the things Dad taught me to do."

They'd reached the part of the property where the groomed trees were planted. They stood in neat rows separated by species. Just beyond the fir trees was Ethan's cabin. He decided to inspect the trees one more time. Maybe a miracle had happened.

Ethan bent down and pulled some needles off one of the trees. As if sensing the importance, George sat down and watched. He examine the needles closely. They were dry, brittle, and a far cry from the lush green foliage they should have been. His last treatment hadn't yielded any improvement.

Ethan's phone rang, jolting him out of his thoughts. The screen flashed with the name of one of his friends—Dave.

"Hey, Dave. What's happening?"

"Hey, Ethan," Dave replied, sounding slightly out of breath. "I just wanted to give you a heads-up. I heard from a reliable source that Mayor Thompson has been contacting other tree farms in the area."

"Really?" Ethan frowned, suddenly very interested. Dave worked in the town hall, and his town gossip was usually reliable. "Has he made any deals with them?"

"I don't think so," Dave said. "But I thought you should know. Is everything okay at your tree farm?"

"Yeah, sure. Probably just a miscommunication. We're good." Ethan hated lying to his friend, but the last thing he needed was the whole town talking about how his tree farm was going under.

"Oh, great. If you need anything, let me know."

"Thanks, Dave," Ethan said, his mind racing. "I appreciate it. I'll straighten things out with the mayor."

As he hung up the phone, Ethan looked around at the trees surrounding him, their branches weighed down by snow and worry.

"All right, George," Ethan said with determination, watching the cat pounce on a leaf. "Let's hope this Ginger person can turn things around."

CHAPTER 8

Ginger stepped out of her car and onto the crisp blanket of snow covering the Woodward farm. Mason had called last night to tell her she had the all-clear to try her solution on the trees. She needed one last piece of information and had chosen to come just past sunrise armed with a thermos of hot coffee and an unyielding determination to get the job done.

She figured she could find her way around without disturbing anyone, especially grumpy Ethan Woodward, so she parked in about the same spot Mason and Kristen had driven her to the day before. She stood looking at the rows of Christmas trees stretched across the land, each one dusted with a delicate layer of frost that sparkled as the first rays of sun began to peek over the horizon.

"Nothing like the scent of fresh pine in the morning," she whispered to herself then inhaled deeply before taking off toward the location of the balsam firs Kristen had shown her the previous day.

As she ventured farther into the trees, Ginger couldn't help but marvel at the peaceful atmosphere surrounding her. The world seemed to hold its breath in anticipation of the day ahead, and she found herself momentarily lost in the beauty of it all. A nearby squirrel chattered its disapproval at her intrusion, snapping her back to reality.

"All right, all right, I'm here for the balsam section, not to disturb your breakfast," she muttered, rolling her eyes at the creature, whose fur was puffed up against the cold, making it look larger than usual.

Ginger almost had her formula perfected. It was a difficult one because she'd needed to add not only the right ingredients to bring the tree back into balance, but also an accelerator so that the tree soaked up the mixture fast. They didn't have long to get the balsams into tip-top shape.

With renewed focus, Ginger made her way to the specific section she'd visited, where the tallest tree stood proudly among its peers. It was now her mission to collect some needles from the very top of the tallest tree. That would provide her with the final piece of information. Too bad she couldn't reach the very top.

"Ten feet," she mused, craning her neck to estimate the height. "Piece of cake." Of course there were shorter trees—she could reach those. The tallest tree was best, though, and Ginger always had to do her best.

She could climb the tree, but since she was prone to be klutzy, that usually never ended well. But... a little way over was a big shed. Maybe there was a ladder inside?

She made her way over and opened the latch. Inside was a rusty plow, shovels, and bags of various fertilizers. A tall ladder leaned against the side wall.

"Jackpot!" she exclaimed, grinning triumphantly. As she approached the ladder, she noticed it seemed to have been untouched for quite some time. She wrangled it out of the shed without too much damage to herself.

"Who needs a gym membership when you've got a ladder workout?" Ginger blew strands of hair out of her face and picked up the ladder. Her arms strained under the weight as she dragged it back to the tree.

"All right, let's do this," she said, placing the ladder against the tall balsam. The branches of the tree kept the ladder from being secure, and it swayed as she stepped onto the first rung.

"Ten feet, nothing to be afraid of," Ginger reassured herself. Ten feet wasn't that high. Probably nothing would happen but a few bruises if she fell. "Just a few more steps, Ginger, you got this."

As she reached the top, the balsam's sweet scent filled her nostrils, conjuring up cozy Christmas visions, but those were short-lived as her clumsy nature reared its head.

"Ooh!" Ginger yelped as the ladder started to lurch. Her foot slipped off the rung, sending her arms flailing in a desperate attempt to regain her balance. Time seemed to slow down as she teetered precariously on the ladder, her heart pounding in her chest like a drum. She reached out to grab a branch to steady herself, but it slid out of her grasp.

"Whoopsie-daisy" was the last thing Ginger managed to utter before she plummeted to the ground. The world seemed to spin around her, and it took an awful long time for her to hit the ground. As soon as she did, an agonizing pain shot through her leg. Ginger's eyes widened in shock as she heard a sickening snap. "Oh no," she gasped. "That can't be good at all." She knew her clumsiness had finally caught up with her—it was just like the time she'd slipped on a banana peel while giving a presentation about plant genomes.

Crap, no one knows I'm out here, she thought bitterly, her vision starting to blur from the excruciating pain. The last thing she remembered seeing was Ethan Woodward running from the side of the shed, his face twisted in an even grumpier expression than usual.

Great, here comes the last person I want to rescue me was her last thought before she passed out.

CHAPTER 9

The scream echoed through the crisp morning air, and Ethan's heart skipped a beat. He abandoned the steaming mug of coffee he had been nursing and sprinted toward the sound.

The scream had come from a woman. *Mom? Kristen? What happened? What in the world were they doing out so early in the morning?* The scream had terrified him. He couldn't risk losing another family member.

He came around the small shed near the balsam firs and saw someone crumpled in the snow next to the tallest tree, a toppled ladder beside her. It wasn't his mother or Kristen. It was Ginger!

He rushed over, knelt beside her, and checked for signs of life. He let out a sigh of relief when he felt her breath on his hand, but his worry didn't dissipate completely. She was pale, the whiteness of her skin making her hair look even more fiery. Her breathing was shallow, and the angle her left leg was bent in made Ethan cringe.

Ginger began to stir, groaning in pain. Her eyes flickered open, and Ethan was momentarily taken aback by the brilliant green color and the flecks of gold that he hadn't noticed yesterday.

"Try not to move," Ethan said as his mind raced ahead, figuring how to get her to the hospital. There was only one ambulance for several towns. It would be faster for him to drive her.

"Ugh... my leg," she mumbled weakly, her face contorted with pain.

"All right, Ginger. Hang in there. We'll get you some help," he reassured her, doing his best to keep his voice steady.

As he carefully lifted her into his arms, trying to avoid causing any further pain, he couldn't help but notice how light she felt. It seemed so strange that someone so full of life could be so fragile in his grasp.

"Okay, here we go," he murmured as he started carrying her toward his truck.

Each step Ethan took elicited a pained "ouch" from Ginger. "Can you take it easy?" she asked, her voice tight with pain. Ethan tried to move more gently, but with every step he took, she squeaked like a toy being squeezed.

The icy terrain made it difficult for Ethan to maintain his balance, and he found himself slipping and sliding like a novice ice skater. Ginger gripped him tighter, her knuckles white with effort. “Maybe we should have called an ambulance.”

“It would take them forever. This will be faster.”

As they continued their awkward trek, a low-hanging branch caught Ethan off guard, smacking him right in the face. He let out a muffled “oof” and stumbled, nearly dropping Ginger in the process.

“Now you’re getting as clumsy as me.” Ginger let out a laugh, which was cut short by a squeal of pain.

Finally, they reached the car, and Ethan managed to get the passenger door open.

“What were you even doing out here this early?” Ethan asked as he gently slid her into the passenger seat of his truck.

“I needed some more pine needles for my experiments, and Mason said I could come,” she mumbled weakly, her face contorted with pain.

“If you’d called me, I could’ve come out to help you.”

Ginger frowned and let out a yelp.

Ethan sensed there was something to her

response, and suddenly, it hit him—he hadn't exactly made her feel welcome when she had been at the farm yesterday. He felt a pang of guilt—if he had been more open and approachable, maybe this accident wouldn't have happened.

"It wouldn't have been a bother." He meant to sound contrite, but it came out rather grumpy even to his own ears.

"It's okay. These things happen to me all the time," Ginger said, smiling through the pain. The warmth of her smile seemed to chase away some of the chill in the air, and Ethan found himself grateful for her ability to find humor even in the most difficult situations.

"All right, let's get you to the hospital," he said, snapping her seatbelt in. Then he jogged over to the driver's side.

CHAPTER 10

Ginger's eyelids fluttered open. The world around her was a blur of sterile white and harsh fluorescent light. She tried to take in her surroundings but felt as though her brain were swimming through a thick fog of pea soup.

"Ugh... where am I?" she groaned, attempting to sit up, only for a sharp pain to shoot through her left leg. "Ow!"

"Hey, hey, easy there." Ethan's voice cut through the haze, his strong hands gently pushing her back against the pillows. "You're in the hospital."

Ginger blinked at him, trying to focus her vision. He looked like he hadn't slept in days, dark circles underlining his eyes, and his usually neatly combed hair was a disheveled mess. Her heart skipped a beat, despite her confusion. Was it possible that the brooding tree farmer had been watching over her?

"Wha... What happened?" she asked, her voice barely above a whisper.

"Remember that little tumble you took on our farm?" Ethan asked, a hint of amusement touching his lips. "Turns out you broke your leg."

"Ah," she replied, feeling her face flush with embarrassment as it all came flooding back to her. "Of course I did. It's not a proper day for Ginger Sanders without an accident, right?"

Ethan chuckled softly. "It seems so. You've been out for a while, which is why I've been here keeping an eye on you."

"Really? You didn't have to do that, you know," Ginger said, touched by his concern. As much as she hated being a damsel in distress, she couldn't help but feel a warm swell in her chest at the thought of the strong, silent Ethan sitting vigil by her bedside.

"Least I could do after you fell on my property," he said.

"Thanks," Ginger murmured. She looked around the room, taking in the sterile space with a pang of loneliness. "I hope you didn't neglect your farm because of me."

"No. We haven't been here that long," he assured her.

"How long?"

"Only a few hours."

That was good. Ginger hated the idea of being unconscious for a long time. And now that she was waking up and starting to feel better, all she wanted was to get out of there.

The door burst open, and Mason walked in with Kristen by his side. Both of them looked a little frazzled, but their faces instantly lit up when they saw Ginger sitting up in bed.

"Hey, look who's awake!" Mason exclaimed, holding up an enormous bouquet of flowers. "We thought we'd come to cheer you up, but it looks like someone beat us to it." He winked playfully at Ethan, who rolled his eyes good-naturedly.

"Guys, you shouldn't have," Ginger said, touched by their thoughtfulness. She inhaled the sweet scent of the flowers before placing them on the bedside table.

"Of course we should!" Kristen chimed in, pulling up a chair and taking Ginger's free hand. "How are you feeling?"

"Better now that you guys are here," Ginger replied honestly. "I guess I had a bit of a rough day."

"Speaking of rough days," Mason began, his eyes twinkling mischievously, "do you remember that time in fourth grade when you tripped on the playground and knocked over the entire row of bikes?"

Ginger groaned, covering her face with her hands. "Oh, no, please don't remind me!"

"Come on, it was hilarious!" Mason insisted, laughing. "You were trying to show off for that new boy—What was his name... Timmy? Tommy? And you ended up causing a bicycle domino effect!"

"His name was Tony, and can we please forget that ever happened?" Ginger pleaded, turning a deep shade of red.

"Aw, don't worry, Ginger," Mason said, leaning in to give her a bear hug. "We love you, clumsiness and all. Plus, it's nice to know some things never change."

"Speaking of things that never change." Ida Green entered the room, carrying a large plate of cookies. "I thought you might be in need of a little sugar boost after your ordeal."

"Ida? How did you even know I was here?" Ginger glanced at Ethan, who shrugged.

"News travels fast in small towns," Kristen said.

"Well, you shouldn't have come all the way down here," Ginger said. "It's just a broken leg. I'm sure I'll be released any minute." She reached for a cookie and eyed the door, hoping for a doctor to come and release her.

The door opened, but it wasn't a doctor. It was Myrtle.

"Ginger! I heard someone was brought in, and I just had to come see who it was. I'm so sorry you got hurt, dear," Myrtle said, her eyes widening at the sight of Ginger's cast.

"Thanks, Myrtle," Ginger replied with a weak smile. "I hope you didn't come all the way here to see me." This was getting ridiculous. Ginger knew Pinecone Falls was a small town, but she barely knew these people.

"Ah, well, I was actually here trying to find someone to foster some kittens," Myrtle admitted. "I figured nurses are so nurturing, I was sure to find a victim... er, volunteer."

"Um, excuse me?" a voice interrupted from the doorway. It was Dorothy, looking apologetic and concerned. "I hope I'm not intruding, but I heard about what happened, and I wanted to come introduce myself. I'm Dorothy Woodward, and I feel absolutely terrible that you fell at the tree farm."

Ginger was touched by the woman's concern. "Please don't worry about it. Accidents happen, especially to me."

"Well, it's nice to meet you. Of course, the circumstances could be better." Dorothy waved to Ginger's cast. "Mason has said wonderful things about you."

Before Ginger could reply, the doctor entered with a clipboard in hand. He looked at Ginger then at the worried faces of her friends and family. "Miss Sanders, you'll be relieved to know that your injury isn't too severe. However, you will need to rent a wheelchair—no walking for at least two weeks due to the nature of the fracture."

"Two weeks?" Ginger's mind raced, adjusting to this news. How would she get around the tree farm? Would she be able to mix up the formula she'd devised for the trees while in a wheelchair?

"Better safe than sorry," the doctor added, his tone a mixture of caution and sympathy. "You don't want to risk further injury."

"Thank you, Doctor," Ginger replied, trying to sound appreciative while secretly cursing her terrible luck. "I promise I'll be careful."

"We'll take another look in a week, and if everything looks good, you can start to use the crutches part-time," the doctor said encouragingly before turning to leave.

Ginger looked around at everyone. "I guess that's not so bad. I'm sure I'll be able to get around fine in the wheelchair, and it's only for a few weeks," she chirped, showing her usual cheery optimism.

"There might be a problem," Ida interjected. "The inn doesn't have an elevator, and there are no rooms downstairs."

"Really?" Ginger gnawed her bottom lip. How would she get upstairs in a wheelchair?

Dorothy stepped forward. "I have that covered. Since you fell on our property, it's only fitting that you stay with us."

Kristen nodded. "I agree, except for one thing. The farmhouse only has bedrooms upstairs."

"Actually... I think I have the perfect solution." Dorothy's eyes slid over to Ethan.

Ginger's gaze followed Dorothy's, her spirits sinking. Hopefully the woman wasn't going to suggest she move in with grumpy Ethan. He had saved her, though. She remembered how his touch had been gentle, and she knew he had been carefully trying not to jostle her, but still, she wasn't going to move in with the guy.

"What?" Ethan looked as if he had no idea what Dorothy was insinuating.

"Your cabin is perfect, dear," Dorothy said. "It's one floor, and Ginger can have privacy and access to the bathroom and kitchen."

"What? It's too small for two of us!" Ethan's eyes darted around the room.

Dorothy shook her head. "I didn't mean for you two to shack up. You move into the farmhouse and let Ginger have the cabin. It's the least we can do."

Ginger blew out a breath. She didn't have many options, and she still wanted to work on the tree solutions. Maybe being on the farm would have advantages. And it was nice of Dorothy to offer.

Everyone in the room seemed to hold their breath, waiting for Ginger's reaction. "Wow, um... that's so generous of you. But I don't want to put anyone out."

"Nonsense!" Dorothy waved her hand, looking far more delighted than Ginger thought was warranted by the circumstances. "You're not putting anyone out, and we'd love to have you. Ethan won't mind. Will you, dear?"

"Of course not, Mom," Ethan agreed, though his expression suggested he felt just as awkward about the idea as Ginger did.

"Perfect," Ginger chirped as she decided to put a positive spin on things. After all, where else could she go?

CHAPTER 11

Ethan leaned against the doorway as he watched his mother, Kristen, and Mason work together to rearrange his cabin. The scene was a flurry of activity, with Kristen and Mason pushing furniture aside while Dorothy directed them like an orchestra conductor. He had mixed feelings. In part, he felt responsible for Ginger's accident, and this really was the best place for her to stay. But the other part of him felt like he was being invaded. He didn't like the idea of someone else touching his things and living in his space.

"All right, now let's move the couch closer to the wall," Dorothy instructed, her hands on her hips as she surveyed the room. "Ginger, wheel yourself over here so we can make sure you can get around."

"Watch out for the coffee table." Ethan lurched toward the table to keep it from tipping over.

"Sorry!" Ginger's face reddened. "I guess I need some more experience with this thing. I promise to be extra careful, though."

His brain had been formulating a sarcastic remark, but when she smiled up at him, he forgot what it was and simply nodded, being careful to arrange his features into a grumpy frown.

Ginger complied with Dorothy's commands eagerly. She maneuvered her wheelchair through the narrow pathways they'd created, her cheeks flushed with excitement. Ethan admired her cheery attitude. This couldn't be easy for her, and judging by the way she winced every so often, she was probably in pain.

"Perfect! Now, let's make sure you can reach everything in the kitchen," Dorothy continued, her voice warm and encouraging.

They followed her into the small cooking area, where she began opening drawers and pulling plates and glasses out of the cabinets. "These should be on the counter for easy access," she said, placing them within Ginger's reach.

"Thank you, Dorothy." Ginger's gratitude was evident. "I really appreciate all of this help."

"It's the least we can do. And don't worry about cooking—I'll bring meals over for you."

"I really don't want you to go to too much trouble," Ginger said. "I can manage just fine. Dr. Lewis told me to stay off my leg ninety percent of the time, but I'm still able to get in and out of bed on my own, and I can make sandwiches and salads, so don't worry about me."

"Okay." Dorothy's expression indicated she was still going to bring over food anyway. "But if you need anything, don't hesitate to ask. We're all here for you."

"Thank you," Ginger said.

In the corner of the room, Kristen and Mason continued to rearrange the furniture, working together seamlessly. At one point, Kristen stumbled over a throw rug, nearly losing her balance. Mason reached out, catching her with a protective arm around her waist.

"Careful there," he teased, his voice warm and affectionate.

"Thanks." Kristen giggled, her cheeks flushing a rosy pink. She looked up at Mason, and their eyes locked for a moment, filled with tenderness and love.

Ethan scowled, but inwardly, he felt a pang of envy and loneliness as he watched their intimate exchange. When had he last experienced that kind of connection with someone? The truth was, it had been a long time since he'd allowed himself to get close to anyone—he was too afraid of vulnerability and loss. But seeing his sister so happy with Mason almost made him long for that missing piece in his life. *Almost.*

Mason glanced over at Ginger. "I hope clumsiness isn't contagious."

"Very funny," Ginger said good-naturedly.

A knock sounded at the door, and Ethan opened it to reveal Ida Green with a giant suitcase and a couple of boxes.

Ginger wheeled around. "Ida! Thank you so much for bringing my stuff."

"It's no trouble." Ida started to lift a box, but Ethan got to it first.

"I'll get this, Ida. You go inside." Ethan hefted the box and grabbed the suitcase handle.

"Could you set the box on the counter?" Ginger asked.

Ethan set it down, and she wheeled over and started to remove things—a microscope, glass slides, beakers, and a Bunsen burner.

"What's all that for?" Ethan asked.

"I'm continuing my research. I'd almost gotten a good formula down when I fell. In fact..." She reached into her pocket, pulled out some pine needles, and held them up. "I have the final piece of the equation right here."

"Really, Ginger, you don't have to work while you're recovering," Dorothy said.

"I appreciate that, but I want to see this through. Besides, it'll give me something to do while I'm stuck inside." Ginger glanced down at the cast on her leg. "I might need some help applying my solution to the trees, though, since I can't get around outside in the snow."

"Of course, dear. I'm sure Ethan will be delighted to help you." Dorothy glanced over at Ethan. "Won't you?"

Ethan's stomach sank at the twinkle in his mother's eyes. Was she trying to fix him up with Ginger? That was *not* going to happen. But it made sense for him to help Ginger—the trees were his responsibility. He would have to help her, but that didn't mean he had to get close to her. In fact, the best thing would be to make her want to spend the least amount of time with him possible.

Ethan set his face into his grumpiest scowl he could muster and met his mother's gaze. "Of course. I want the trees to be healthy more than anything."

"Good, then it's settled." Dorothy clapped her hands together.

Ethan grunted and picked up the box he'd set near the door. Earlier, he'd thrown some of his clothes and toiletries into the box. "Better get my room set up," he mumbled as he headed out the door.

The prospect of spending the next few weeks in his childhood bedroom in the farmhouse was not very appealing, but it was better than spending them in his tiny cabin with Ginger.

CHAPTER 12

Ginger hummed a cheerful tune as she wheeled herself closer to the makeshift lab station in Ethan's cabin. The sun streamed through the window, casting a warm glow over the various scientific instruments scattered about. Despite her unfortunate injury, Ginger couldn't help but feel cheery. After all, she was doing what she loved most—saving plants.

"All right, my little pine needles," she whispered affectionately, adjusting the microscope's focus. "Let's see what we can do for you."

As Ginger peered into the eyepiece, she immediately noticed the telltale signs of nitrate deficiency in the balsam fir samples. *Good, one piece of the puzzle solved. Now how to get the appropriate nutrients into the trees quickly.*

Her brow furrowed in concentration, she began brainstorming potential solutions, her pencil flying across the pages of her notebook. Time was of the essence, and with the ground being frozen, soil amendment would be difficult. Besides, that usually didn't work as well or as fast on full-grown trees.

"Okay, so we could try adding a nitrogen-rich solution directly to the leaves," she mused aloud, adding the idea to her list. "Or perhaps some sort of compost tea? Or maybe..."

She trailed off, realizing that she needed to consult one of her favorite books. She wheeled over to a side table, where Ethan had stacked her reference books. She reached over to dig through the books.

"Ah-ha! There you are!" Ginger exclaimed triumphantly as her hand closed around the spine of the well-worn text. In her excitement, however, she knocked over a silver frame with a photo in it. The frame teetered on the edge of the table, and Ginger dropped her book to rescue it before it fell to the floor.

Placing it back on the table, she noticed the photo was a picture of two men standing in front of a row of young fir trees. One was a younger version of Ethan, and the other an older version of him.

That must be his father, she thought as she pushed it a safe distance from the edge. Glancing around the room, she realized what had seemed odd about the cabin—there were no other pictures, knickknacks, or decorative items. It spoke volumes that Ethan kept out only this one picture of him and his dad. She knew his dad had died about a year ago, and her heart broke a little for him. It was obvious in the picture how close the two had been.

That might explain why Ethan acted so grumpy all the time. And Mason had mentioned something about his wife passing away too. No wonder the guy was so sad. Well, the nicest thing she could do was help him get the balsam firs in tip-top shape. Now, she was more determined than ever.

As she wheeled back to the counter with the book, she noticed again how sparse the cabin was. It was the opposite of the farmhouse, which she'd seen briefly after Mason and Kristen had driven her back from the hospital. The farmhouse brimmed with warmth and cheer, every surface adorned with festive Christmas decorations. Even now, the image of the twinkling lights and colorful baubles Dorothy had set out filled Ginger's heart with joy.

"Maybe I should get a little tree to decorate in here," she mused, a small smile creeping onto her face as she imagined how much it would brighten the cabin. “I need some holiday spirit.”

With a determined nod, Ginger cracked open her book, eager to come up with the final solution for the trees.

“All right, let’s see what you’ve got for me,” she whispered to the book, her eyes scanning the text with a laser-like focus. “We’re going to save those trees, one way or another.”

CHAPTER 13

The farmhouse is cluttered with holiday cheer, Ethan thought grumpily as he stood at the top of the stairs, his hand resting on the wooden banister worn smooth by generations of Woodwards. He supposed the excessive decorating his mother had done was cheery, but he preferred the simple decor in his cabin. Okay, maybe he had to admit the cabin was a bit bare; perhaps something in between the farmhouse and the cabin would be ideal.

He'd just finished unpacking his few belongings in his childhood bedroom, and he couldn't decide if it was more depressing or comforting to be back here. So many memories were tied up within these walls—the laughter-filled Christmases with his father and the bittersweet moments spent with his late wife. At least it would only be for a short time, he reminded himself.

As he descended the stairs, his hand accidentally knocked one of the ornaments off the garland draped around the banister. It tumbled down the steps. He rushed to catch it before it could smashed to pieces.

"Maybe klutziness *is* contagious," he thought to himself as he grabbed the ornament. Images of Ginger in his cabin bubbled up. He'd snuck a peek back in as he left, and the scene had looked cozy with his mom, Kristen, Mason, and Ida gathered around Ginger. She seemed to add warmth to the cabin. It almost seemed *right* for her to be there, and the thought scared Ethan for some reason.

As he crouched to get the ornament, the soft sound of paws against floorboards startled him from his thoughts as George came skulking toward him, his green eyes filled with curiosity and maybe even a bit of sympathy. Smiling softly to himself, Ethan reached out and petted the cat quietly, making sure no one was around to see him.

The aroma of caramelized onions and sautéed garlic mingling with a hint of rosemary and thyme wafted out from the kitchen. That was one benefit to being back in the farmhouse—his mom's delicious cooking.

Ethan headed toward the kitchen.

"There you are." Dorothy turned from the pot she was stirring. "Did you get settled in your room?"

"Sure did. It's kind of weird being back in there, but seems like it's for the best."

"And it's only for a little while." Dorothy returned her attention to the pot.

"Where is Kristen?" Ethan asked.

"She and Mason went out to dinner." Dorothy turned off the burner.

"All the more for me." Ethan tried to sneak a peek at the pot his mother was guarding so closely. "And if I know you, Mom, it's bound to be something amazing."

Dorothy swatted his hand away from the pot with a gentle laugh. "It's your favorite."

"Beef stew?" Ethan's mouth started to water. "I'll set the table."

Dorothy chuckled softly. "Oh, that won't be necessary, dear."

"Really?" Ethan asked, pausing midmotion with a fork in one hand and a napkin in the other. "Why not?"

"Because," Dorothy said, her voice taking on a mischievous lilt, "we're going to take this meal over to Ginger at the cabin."

Ethan's stomach plummeted at the words. He had

been so focused on the tantalizing smells of his favorite meal that he'd momentarily forgotten about the determined plant specialist currently occupying his cabin. And now he had to have dinner with her?

Dorothy turned around, her eyes sparkling. "What you *can* do, though, is help me pack this stuff up so we can get it over there while it's still hot."

CHAPTER 14

"Let me help you set the table." Ginger wheeled herself from the kitchen to the table and began arranging knives, forks, and spoons, humming as she worked.

The mouthwatering aroma of Dorothy's homemade beef stew and freshly baked rolls filled the air, and her stomach rumbled in anticipation. She'd been surprised and delighted that Dorothy had brought her homemade beef stew and rolls and even more surprised that Ethan had come with her, although she suspected his growling stomach might have been his main motivation.

"You don't need to do a thing, dear. Just sit," Dorothy insisted, placing a steaming bowl on the table.

Ethan was quiet, nodding responses and avoiding eye contact. Yesterday, she would have put it down to him being a grump, but after seeing the picture of him and his father, she couldn't help but feel a deeper understanding of Ethan's reserved demeanor. Beneath his gruff exterior, she sensed a kind-hearted person whose emotions ran deep.

As they enjoyed the dinner, Dorothy and Ginger engaged in lively conversation, with Ethan occasionally offering a comment.

"This stew is amazing." Ginger spooned up a chunk of potato from the thick stew and brought it to her mouth, trying to keep it from dripping on her shirt. "It's so flavorful. What's your secret?"

Dorothy smiled, clearly pleased with the compliment. "Well, to start I sear the beef. It locks in the juices and gives the meat a wonderful texture." She leaned in slightly, as if sharing a treasured secret. "But the real secret is in the spices."

"Oh? Do tell."

"I use a mix of oregano, basil, rosemary, and parsley to create that classic, comforting taste. Then I add a bit of paprika and cayenne pepper to give it a subtle kick, while celery seed and onion powder enhance the natural flavors of the vegetables. And, of course, I season it with salt and pepper to taste," Dorothy said with a touch of pride in her voice.

"It's outstanding. I think I need the recipe."

"I'll write it down for you." Dorothy dabbed her mouth with a napkin before continuing, "Enough about me. Ginger, tell me about your family."

Ginger hesitated for a moment then replied, "Well, we aren't that close. Everyone's spread out across the country, so we don't see each other often."

"And do you all get together for Christmas?" Dorothy inquired, her eyes filled with genuine curiosity.

Ginger shrugged, a hint of longing in her voice. "Sometimes, but it's usually in the Caribbean. I wanted something different this year, some snow and a traditional Christmas."

Dorothy glanced around the cabin, a slight frown creasing her brow. "You know, there aren't any Christmas decorations in here. Maybe I can help with that, give you the real feeling of the holiday season."

Ginger's eyes brightened at the suggestion. "That sounds wonderful, Dorothy. Thank you."

Dorothy turned to her son with a mischievous smile. "We can get one of the small trees from the lot."

Ethan, who had been quietly listening to the

conversation, looked up in surprise. "A tree? I don't think one will fit."

"Just a small one. It would fit perfectly on that table by the window," Dorothy insisted, a determined twinkle in her eye. "It wouldn't be a traditional Christmas without one."

Ethan hesitated then finally nodded. "Sure. We have plenty of smaller spruces that are in good shape."

Ginger was heartened at Dorothy's thoughtfulness. She felt a sense of belonging she hadn't experienced in years. The warmth of the cabin, the hearty stew, and the snowflakes dancing outside the window all seemed to weave a spell of contentment around her, allowing her to appreciate the simple joys of sharing a meal with new friends despite the fact that her leg ached.

The spell was broken by a knock at the door.

"I'll get it." Dorothy placed a hand on Ginger's shoulder and walked the short distance to the door.

It was a tall, portly man with graying hair and a neatly trimmed beard. He was dressed in a suit despite the late hour.

"Mayor Thompson." Dorothy sounded surprised. "What brings you here at suppertime?"

Ginger sensed a hint of history in Dorothy's voice, as if the mayor was an old friend that hadn't kept in touch. Probably something to do with Ethan's father's death, Ginger surmised. It would make sense a prominent businessman like Ethan's dad would know the mayor.

"I'm sorry I haven't visited in some time, Dorothy. I saw the lights on and thought I'd get an update on the tree for the Christmas Eve lighting." The mayor's tone was somewhat apologetic but also tinged with authority as his gaze slid over Dorothy's shoulder to Ethan, who had come to stand behind his mother. "I've been in communication with Ethan as I used to do with Charlie. I thought I would stop by and maybe get a look at the tree for the Christmas Eve lighting. I've made some calls to other tree farms, so if the Woodwards won't have a tree for the lighting—"

Ginger wheeled over abruptly, knocking into a side table and almost toppling a lamp, which Ethan deftly caught. Her action stopped the mayor midsentence.

"Good evening, Mayor. I'm *Dr.* Sanders." She emphasized the word "doctor" and held out her hand. It hadn't taken her long to figure out what was going on here. Everyone knew balsams were the epitome of Christmas trees. Apparently the mayor had previously wanted to see a tree, but since the balsams were the ones with the problem, Ethan had been reluctant to show him one. She wasn't about to let the mayor bully the Woodwards.

Mayor Thompson's left brow rose. "Doctor? Is someone ill?"

Ginger smiled up at him. "Not that kind of doctor. PhD. I'm a tree scientist."

"Oh." Mayor Thompson looked like he wasn't sure what to say, so Ginger continued. "I'm an expert on fir trees. The Woodwards have hired me to make sure all the trees are in tip-top shape, including the perfect balsam for the tree lighting."

Ethan and Dorothy exchanged surprised glances but quickly played along. "That's right, Mayor. We're all working together to make sure this year's tree is the best," Dorothy chimed in with a reassuring smile. "It's the least we can do to honor Charlie."

"Oh. Then you have one picked out?" the mayor asked.

"Yes," Ginger answered quickly. "But you can't see it yet. I'm treating it with exomethachloride to bring out the lush green of the leaves, and it's got goop all over it."

The mayor furrowed his brow but eventually nodded, his skepticism giving way to cautious optimism. "I'll be looking forward to seeing the tree some other time, then," he said before departing.

With the door closed behind the mayor, Ginger turned to Ethan and Dorothy and let out her breath. “Well, that went well, I think.”

“You were brilliant!” Dorothy said.

“What’s exomethachloride?” Ethan asked.

Ginger shrugged. “I made it up. It was the first thing I could think of to get rid of him.”

Dorothy laughed. “Quick thinking, but he’s still a problem. He’ll be wanting to see that tree sooner rather than later.”

“I know,” Ginger said, feeling an exciting sense of camaraderie with Ethan and Dorothy. “That’s why I’m glad that I think I have found the perfect solution to get those trees healthy well before Christmas Eve.”

CHAPTER 15

Ethan snuck glances at Ginger as they worked together to clear the table. It was clear to see she was very passionate about her work as she filled them in on her research, pointing out the makeshift lab she'd set up on the counter. Her microscope, beakers, and various scientific instruments were neatly arranged, a testament to her dedication to her work.

"I've been studying the needles," Ginger explained, indicating the slides under the microscope. "And I found that they need more nitrogen. I believe I've devised a formula and method that will help the trees absorb it more efficiently, which means they should be looking good in about five days."

Dorothy's eyes sparkled with delight. "That's fantastic news, Ginger!"

Ethan watched in fascination. When Ginger talked about her work, she became so animated, her cheeks flushed and her eyes bright. She looked beautiful. Their eyes locked for a brief moment, and he quickly looked away. It wouldn't do to get too close to her. That might lead to heartbreak, and Ethan had had enough of that for one lifetime. Even so, he was grateful she'd found something they could try.

She continued, "The solution needs to be applied in a specific way to ensure its effectiveness, and I'm going to need a few things."

"Anything," Dorothy said. "We'll get you whatever you need."

"Okay, they might sound strange. I need about eight cups of coffee grounds, a dozen eggshells, and some manure. Oh! And if you can find some banana peels, that would be a bonus." Ginger looked at them. "And some type of syringe that can penetrate the bark. I think we need to inject the solution directly into the roots of the trees."

Ethan couldn't keep the frown off his face. Coffee grounds? Banana peels? Now he was starting to think that maybe this woman was some kind of quack. But

Mason swore she could work wonders, and since he didn't have a better option, he supposed he'd go along.

Before they could discuss the application process further, another knock came at the door. Dorothy went to answer it.

"Well, it seems like we have a lot of visitors tonight," Ginger remarked with a smile, breaking the silence.

"Usually, no one comes here."

Ethan glanced at the door to see Myrtle from the animal rescue. Judging by the tote bag full of yarn and knitting needles, she wasn't here to see *him*.

Myrtle stepped into the cabin, the colorful assortment of yarn practically spilling out of the bag. "The knitting club at the Cozy Holly Inn thought Ginger might appreciate something to help pass the time while she's here," Myrtle explained with a warm smile.

Ginger's face lit up with gratitude as she reached out to accept the bag. "Thank you so much!" She rummaged through the bag. "It's perfect. Please thank everyone for me."

"You're very welcome." Myrtle reached down and picked up a plastic carrier.

"What's in there?" Dorothy asked, craning her neck for a better look.

Ethan had a pretty good idea, considering the mewling sounds coming out of it.

Myrtle beamed with pride as she opened the carrier to reveal three adorable orange-striped kittens. "I was hoping Ginger might be willing to foster these little ones while she's here," she said. "Since she's all alone in the cabin, they could keep her company and give her something to care for."

Ethan's mind raced with images of kittens creating chaos in his once-peaceful cabin, litter boxes occupying valuable space, and cat hair blanketing every surface. He tried to think of a polite way to decline the offer, but before he could voice his concerns, Dorothy interjected with enthusiasm.

"That's a wonderful idea, Myrtle! They'll be perfect companions for Ginger."

Ginger's eyes filled with adoration for the tiny feline she'd taken out of the carrier and was now cradling under her chin. "I'd love to have them here, but this is Ethan's place. It's ultimately his decision."

Ethan attempted a feeble protest, saying, "It might be too much for Ginger to handle on top of her recovery..." But his words faltered as he saw the joy in her eyes as she cuddled the kittens. And he had to admit they were kind of cute.

Sighing in resignation, he finally nodded his approval. “All right, they can stay.”

With the kittens’ arrival now sanctioned, the three women quickly got down to business, discussing knitting patterns and other topics that Ethan had zero interest in. He saw his cue and said his farewells, heading back to the farmhouse, his mind whirling with ideas of where he could get all of the items Ginger needed for her tree-saving plan.

CHAPTER 16

"Want a banana?" Dorothy mumbled the words around a mouthful of banana as she held one out to Ethan. It was the next morning, and Ethan had woken up with a fresh sense of purpose and hopefulness.

He glanced at the pile of banana peels on the counter. "How many of those have you eaten?"

"This is my third. Ginger said she needed the peels."

"How many more do you think we need to eat to get enough peels?"

Dorothy pretended to ponder the question. "Hmm, maybe another dozen or two? They're good for you."

They shared a laugh before Ethan turned serious, thinking about the rest of the items on the list. "I'm going to get the other ingredients for Ginger today. I'll hit up my buddy Tommy for the manure since he owns a dairy farm. Maybe he'll have a syringe as well. But where can I find a pound of coffee grounds?"

Dorothy's eyes lit up as she had an idea. "Why don't you try the Pinecone Falls Café? They make a lot of coffee every day. I'm sure they'll have plenty of grounds to spare."

"Excellent idea." Ethan grabbed his coat and another banana. "See you when I get back."

As he drove through Pinecone Falls, he felt a tinge of joy at the holiday decor. Just a tinge, but it was something he hadn't felt in years. In fact, the holidays usually made him more depressed than anything. Maybe he was emerging from the shadow of grief that had followed him around for the past years.

The town had a reputation as a Christmas destination, and everyone liked to play that up to make the tourists as happy as they could during the season. Festive wreaths made of evergreen boughs and red velvet bows hung from the lampposts, while twinkling fairy lights draped the storefronts, casting a warm, welcoming glow on the snow-covered sidewalks. The entire scene looked like something straight out of a classic holiday movie, evoking a sense of nostalgia and warmth in everyone who passed through.

Ethan actually had a smile on his face as he glanced toward the town square with its sparkling ice sculptures, fanciful snowmen, and glittering lights... until his gaze landed on the empty spot in the middle, where the mayor was expecting a Woodward balsam fir to be standing very soon.

He'd better get a move on; time was of the essence. He pulled into a spot in front of the Pinecone Falls Café, got out of the truck, and took a deep breath of crisp winter air before heading toward the café. He'd called the owner, Lucy, on his way, and she was getting the coffee grounds together for him.

Luckily, she had more than he needed, and she also hadn't asked why he needed them, which was good. He didn't want it getting around town that he was desperately trying to make the trees healthy.

The charming little café was a local favorite known for its delicious pastries and homestyle cooking. The exterior was just as festive as the rest of the town, with its holly-covered windows and icicle lights dripping from the green awning, enticing passersby to come in and warm themselves with a steaming cup of coffee.

He pulled open the door and was greeted with a pleasant aroma of brewed coffee and fresh-baked bread. He heard the sound of cutlery clinking against plates and the low murmur of conversations in the background. Hopefully, no one he knew was here, and he could get his coffee grounds and get out before anyone asked any questions.

He had almost made it to the counter when someone called out his name. “Ethan! Hey!”

He turned around to see Kristen sitting at a table with her friends Julie and Ivy. He groaned inwardly. He couldn’t avoid them now.

“Hey, Kristen,” he said, forcing a smile. “What are you guys up to?”

“Just grabbing some coffee,” Kristen said, gesturing to the cups on the table. “What about you?”

“Same.” Ethan moved toward the counter, hoping that would be enough to get him out of the conversation. But of course, it wasn’t.

“I heard you had a new guest at your cabin?” Ivy wiggled her eyebrows, and Ethan frowned at Kristen. What had her sister been telling them?

“She’s not really my guest. She’s staying at my cabin, but I’ve moved into the farmhouse with Mom and Kristen,” Ethan said.

Ivy took a sip of her coffee and said, “It’s really nice of you guys to put her up, you know.” She took a bite of her chocolate chip muffin, the crumbs falling onto the plate.

Kristen nodded, her mouth full of blueberry muffin. She swallowed before responding, “Well, it’s the least we can do since Ginger broke her leg at our place.”

Julie, who had been busy enjoying her cranberry-orange muffin, looked up with curiosity. “What was she doing there, anyway?”

Kristen and Ethan exchanged a glance, both aware they didn’t want the real reason to be known. Kristen quickly came up with a plausible explanation. “Oh, Ginger’s best friends with Mason, and he wanted to show her around the farm. It was just a freak accident.”

Lucy appeared at Mason’s side, holding a large brown paper bag. She leaned in to speak, and he quickly coughed loudly to cover her words. He didn’t need anyone asking why he was picking up a huge bag of coffee grounds.

“Thanks!” Ethan said a bit too cheerily as he grabbed the bag from her. “What do I owe you?”

She waved him off, smiling warmly. “Oh, don’t worry about it, Ethan. I couldn’t possibly charge you for that.”

“Oh. Well, thanks.”

He glanced back at the table where Julie, Ivy, and Kirsten sat, watching him with curiosity.

Julie was the first to speak. "No charge? That looks like a lot of coffee."

Ivy leaned forward, looking interested. "What do you need all that for? Don't you live alone?"

Ethan hesitated. "Yeah, but, uhhh, I like to drink a lot of coffee."

Julie looked confused. "I didn't even realize that Lucy sold the coffee beans. That's kind of odd, isn't it?"

Kristen jumped in. "Not at all. She buys in bulk."

There was a moment of silence as Ivy and Julie looked at Ethan skeptically. Ethan could feel his cover being blown.

Thankfully, Kristen jumped to his rescue. "Well, we won't keep you from your day. I know you have a lot to do at the tree farm."

"And a lot of coffee to drink," Ivy added.

Everyone cracked up laughing, and Ethan bid them farewell then hurried out of there before anyone could dig too much into what he really had in the bag.

❄

JULIE TOOK a sip of her coffee. "You know, I think that's the most I've seen Ethan talk in, well, ages."

"Maybe even since high school," Ivy chimed in,

taking a bite of her muffin. "He seemed... happier somehow."

Kristen nodded, running her finger around the rim of her cup. "Yeah, it's been tough for him since Sarah passed away." She thought about her brother, his usual brooding demeanor, and how he'd actually cracked a smile or two during their chat.

"Understandably so," Julie agreed, a hint of sadness in her voice. "But I hope he's finding his way to a better place now."

"Me too," Ivy added, reaching across the table to give Kristen's hand a reassuring squeeze. "You've done a great job supporting him, Kristen."

"Thanks." Kristen smiled. "I'm trying my best." She knew Ethan was still struggling, but she also felt a flicker of hope seeing him like this today.

Julie pinched off a corner of her muffin and popped it into her mouth. "My grandmother was asking about getting one of your balsam firs for our Christmas Eve party at the Cozy Holly Inn. But when I stopped by the tree lot earlier, you guys were all out. Are you already sold out for the season?"

Kristen's heart clenched at the mention of the trees. Her fingers crossed under the table, she forced a smile onto her face. "Oh, don't worry, Julie. It's just temporary. Ethan's going to get more trees in plenty of time for the party."

"Really?" Julie asked, relieved. "That's great news! My grandmother would be heartbroken if we didn't have a Woodward balsam for the party."

"Don't worry," Kristen assured her, trying to sound as casual as possible.

"Speaking of Christmas fun," Julie chimed in, her eyes lighting up with excitement, "we should all go ice-skating at the pond this weekend! Nolan has been asking to go. What do you guys think?"

"Ooh, that sounds like a blast!" Ivy agreed, clapping her hands together with enthusiasm. "Count us in!"

Kristen grinned, unable to resist the infectious joy of her friends. "Yeah, let's do it!"

"Great idea!" Ivy said, already pulling out her phone to check her calendar. "How about Saturday afternoon? I'm free then."

"Saturday works for me," Kristen confirmed, already imagining the picturesque scene of them all bundled up in their winter gear, skates slung over their shoulders as they made their way to the pond. She loved the skating pond with its firepits and hot chocolate stands. "I think Mason is free too."

"Hopefully, Mason can stay upright this time around," Julie joked.

The girls burst into laughter. Mason didn't know how to skate and had spent more time on his backside than on his feet at the annual skating party last week. That was okay with Kristen, since one of those falls had initiated their first kiss. She couldn't help but smile at the memory.

As the trio discussed the details of their upcoming outing, Kristen felt a sense of contentment settle over her, despite the looming issue with the trees. She knew Ginger had identified a solution, and Ethan was gathering the ingredients. Hopefully, everything would work out.

CHAPTER 17

Ginger pressed down on the marble pestle, grinding the eggshells in the mortar into a fine powder, her wheelchair parked in front of the kitchen counter. The cozy cabin was filled with the bubbling and hissing of beakers, their contents swirling and changing colors like magical potions. The air was thick with the comforting aroma of coffee and bananas, an odd combination that surprisingly worked.

"Look what I've got!" Dorothy announced as she came through the door with a small three-foot blue spruce Christmas tree. It was perfect—compact enough to fit in the cabin without taking up too much space but big enough to fill the room with festive cheer.

Ginger wheeled herself around to face Dorothy, nearly knocking over a precarious beaker in the process. “Oh, it’s beautiful! Thank you so much!” she gushed, her eyes sparkling with excitement.

The three orange kittens seemed to agree, scampering over to Dorothy as if the tree were a magnet for feline affection.

“You’re very welcome.” Dorothy beamed, setting the tree down on the floor. She scooped up one of the kittens and held it close to her chest. “How are these little guys doing?”

“They get into everything. But they are fun and good company.”

“It doesn’t get much better. George is grown up but still gets into things.” Dorothy laughed. “Let’s get this tree set up. I brought a stand and a tree skirt.”

With a final pat on the kitten’s head, she set it back down and began arranging the tree in front of the window. The sunlight streaming in cast a warm glow on the branches, making Ginger feel even more at home in the inviting cabin.

As Ginger helped Dorothy get the tree in place, she filled her in on her progress with the solution. “Ethan is going to come back later to get the finished solution and apply it to the trees. He dropped off the ingredients earlier, and I'm almost done. He seemed grumpy about the kittens, so he basically handed off the ingredients and ran out." She chuckled at the memory. "I have a feeling he secretly likes them, though."

Dorothy raised a knowing eyebrow as she tightened the screws on the stand to straighten the tree. "Oh, I don't doubt that for a second. I've caught him patting George when he thinks no one's looking."

Ginger grinned. She understood why Ethan would be reluctant to open up even to cats. "Must've been hard on Ethan, losing his wife so young and then his dad."

Dorothy paused and sighed, nodding in agreement. "Yes, it was. But maybe things are getting better now." A mischievous glint flickered in her eyes, but before Ginger could probe further, Dorothy resumed her task, unfurling a festive tree skirt around the base of the small spruce.

Dorothy stepped back to admire their handiwork. "Needs ornaments. I'll get some ornaments from the attic later."

"I have something we can put on it now." Ginger wheeled herself over to her knitting bag and pulled out two glittery white yarn snowflakes she'd crafted earlier. She carefully placed one on the tree and handed the other to Dorothy. "I made this one for you."

Dorothy's eyes lit up with delight as she accepted the snowflake. "Thank you. It's beautiful." She glanced down at Ginger's knitting bag. "I've been knitting something for you too. A scarf, but it's not quite done yet. It's lavender, which I think will be beautiful with your coloring."

Ginger had seen the scarves she'd made for the others. They were lopsided and riddled with holes. But it was a kind gesture, and she'd wear the scarf proudly. "That's really nice of you."

"Okay, well, I better let you get back to work." Dorothy glanced over at the beakers, scooped up one of the kittens, and held it up to look it in the eye. "You be good for Ginger."

She handed the kitten to Ginger and shrugged on her coat. Ginger wheeled over to the door to see her out. "Thanks for the tree."

"You're very welcome!" Dorothy called over her shoulder as she headed off through the woods.

Ginger petted the kitten as she watched Dorothy crunch through the snow. Despite Dorothy's happy demeanor, Ginger had noticed the tight lines that had etched themselves onto Dorothy's face when she'd glanced at the still-bubbling solution. A lot was riding on her success, for not only the balsam fir trees but also the entire Woodward family.

Ginger placed the kitten on the floor with the others and wheeled back to the counter. With one last deep breath, she gave the solution a final stir then leaned back in her chair, saying a silent prayer that her concoction would work.

CHAPTER 18

The savory smell of home cooking drew Ethan toward the kitchen. He wondered what his mother was making for supper. It smelled like a chicken pot pie. He sure hoped it was.

But when he got to the kitchen, he stopped short. He'd expected to find the familiar sight of his mother bustling around the table, pots and pans bubbling away. Instead, his mother was standing by the kitchen table, her coat already on, busily packing a picnic basket.

On seeing him, she looked up and smiled. "Oh, there you are, dear. I'm late for the knitting club and was hoping you could take this down to Ginger." She pointed to the picnic basket and an old cardboard box that sat next to it.

Ethan stood motionless as he tried to adjust to the new plan. He hadn't intended to bring anything. That would involve going inside. He'd been sort of hoping he could just grab the tree solution from her and get to applying it as quickly as possible. But he supposed this was a small favor he could do for his mother since he was going to the cabin anyway.

"Okay, no problem." Ethan glanced at George, who had been sitting in the corner, cleaning his tail. He swore the cat had a smirk on his face. "What's in the box?"

"Some old ornaments. I brought Ginger a tree from the tree lot today, and it needs some ornaments, so I figured she could use these old ones."

Ethan stooped to pick up the picnic basket and the cardboard box. Struggling to balance the two, he headed out the door. "Have a good time, and try not to knit me anything too embarrassing, okay?" he called over his shoulder, only half-joking.

As he trudged toward his truck, he could feel George's eyes following him from the window. He looked back at the house, and there George was, watching out the back window. He could have sworn the cat's smirk grew even wider.

When he arrived at the cabin, he knocked on the door, balancing the items in his arms.

Ginger opened the door, looking surprised. "I didn't realize you'd be bringing things over."

"My mom sent some food." Ethan held out the picnic basket, and Ginger took it then motioned for him to come inside.

"The solution for the trees will be done in just ten more minutes." Ginger peeked into the picnic basket. "Oh wow, it smells delicious! What's in here?"

"I'm not sure. I think it's chicken pot pie."

Ginger's gaze drifted to the box Ethan was still holding. "What's in there?"

"Ornaments," he replied, opening the box to reveal an assortment of colorful, glittering decorations. "Mom thought your tree needed some trimming."

Ginger's face lit up. "Oh, this is perfect! I actually haven't decorated a tree in years, believe it or not."

Neither had Ethan, though he didn't say so.

Ginger set the picnic basket on the table and grabbed the box from him. After setting it in her lap, she opened the top and started pulling out ornaments. Ethan found himself smiling at her enthusiasm, but he quickly rearranged his face into his grumpy expression.

Ethan leaned against the wall, arms crossed, and watched Ginger take the ornaments out of the box. She held them delicately, as if they were precious jewels, and Ethan could see why. They were older ones he remembered from his childhood. He had forgotten about them until now.

"That one," he said, pointing to a red-and-green-striped ball. "My sister and I fought over who got to put it on the tree every year."

Ginger grinned and hung it on a branch. "I can see why. It's lovely."

They continued like that, Ethan describing something he remembered about each ornament as Ginger placed it on the tree—the glass icicles that always made him nervous as a child, the felt Santa Claus that was starting to show its age, and the angel with a broken wing that his mother had always said added character to the tree.

As they worked, Even found himself reliving his childhood through the ornaments. The memories came flooding back, and he couldn't help but smile. Ginger turned on some music, and the sound of Christmas carols filled the air. The scent of pine needles from the tree made it feel like the perfect holiday scene.

As they admired the ornaments, the three orange kittens scampered around Ethan's feet, their playful antics causing him to chuckle. Without thinking, he bent down to pet them, momentarily forgetting his grumpy façade. Luckily, Ginger was too preoccupied with the ornaments to notice.

She wheeled over to the tree, her eyes gleaming with excitement. As she tried to hang a glitter-covered ornament on a branch, it quickly became apparent that her wheelchair made it difficult to reach the tree properly. Ethan, seeing her struggle, rushed over to help her without a second thought.

"Here, let me give you a hand," he offered, taking the ornament from her and placing it on the branch.

"Thanks, Ethan," Ginger said gratefully, handing him another ornament and wheeling around to find the perfect spot for it.

The kittens' playful antics underfoot had become increasingly chaotic. Suddenly, one of them shot out in front of Ginger's path. She lurched the chair sideways, bumping into the table that held the tree.

The tree started to lean...

Ethan's reflexes kicked in, and he lunged to grab the tree before it toppled. As he secured it, he found himself face-to-face with Ginger, their noses mere inches apart.

Ethan's heart raced, and for a brief moment, he pictured himself leaning in for a kiss. But just as quickly as the thought had come, he jumped back, his eyes wide with surprise. What was he thinking? He didn't want to get involved, did he?

The spell of the scene was broken, and the cozy, intimate atmosphere had dissipated. Ethan cleared his throat, trying to regain his composure. "Uh, I should get that solution out to the trees," he stammered, his cheeks flushing with embarrassment.

Ginger, seemingly unaware of the moment they'd almost shared, nodded in agreement. "Of course, I'll grab it for you. We don't want to waste any more time."

Ethan breathed a sigh of relief, grateful for the return to normalcy. As he prepared to head out to the trees, he couldn't help but wonder what had come over him. Was it the holiday spirit, or was it something more?

Ethan stepped out into the cold, crisp night, bundled up in his down jacket. The moon and stars cast a silvery glow across the snow-covered landscape, and the haunting calls of owls echoed through the frosty air. As he breathed, his breath fogged up in front of his face, a testament to the frigid temperatures. The warmth of the cottage seemed a distant memory as he crunched through the snow on the tree farm, a bucket of Ginger's serum and several large garden syringes in hand.

Following Ginger's instructions, Ethan set about

applying the solution directly to the roots of the balsam fir trees, injecting life back into the struggling grove. As he worked, he couldn't help but pause at one particular spot—a place he and Sarah had considered their special hideaway. In the past, a pair of birds had made their home in the nesting box that hung nearby and had returned year after year.

This year, though, the birds hadn't used the nesting box. The birds had moved on, perhaps finding a new place to call home. As he stood there, taking in the change, he realized that maybe it was time for him to move on too. Instead of feeling sad at the thought, a sense of peace washed over him. It was as if he had finally found the missing piece that he'd been searching for. He was healed, and it was time to start living again.

With renewed determination, Ethan continued to apply the serum to the trees, feeling a kinship with the balsams. Just as they needed this chance to become healthy and strong once more, he, too, needed to embrace the opportunity to grow and find happiness again. He only wished he'd stayed at the cabin long enough to find out what was in that picnic basket his mother had sent over.

CHAPTER 19

The next morning, Kristen and Mason knocked on the door of the cabin, ready to take Ginger to her doctor's appointment. Ginger hobbled to the car on her crutches. Her broken leg was still mending, but the pain was becoming more manageable each day.

"Hopefully things have healed enough so you can spend more time on the crutches," Kristen said cheerfully as Mason helped Ginger into the passenger seat of their truck. "Winter makes it hard to get around with just the wheelchair."

"You can say that again," Ginger said. "I'm getting cabin fever being stuck inside. And I want to check on those balsam firs as soon as possible."

Kristen waved her hand. "Don't you worry about

that now. Mason and I thought we'd take you on a fun outing after your appointment."

"An...outing?" Ginger asked hesitantly. She didn't want to be an inconvenience in her condition.

"You'll see," Mason said with a grin as he put the truck in gear.

A few hours later, Ginger had her marching orders from the doctor as she sat snugly under a heavy wool blanket in a large sleigh gliding over the snowy woods. Kristen and Mason had brought her to the family farm of Mason's friend Nolan. They offered scenic sleigh rides along wooded trails. The horses' hooves and jingling sleigh bells were the only sounds as sunlight filtered through snow-dusted pines.

"This is magical," Ginger breathed, feeling her stress melt away. "Thank you both. And thanks for taking me to the doctors."

Kristen squeezed Ginger's arm affectionately. "You needed a break from reality for a while. And it's the least we could do after you came to save Woodward Farm's Christmas tree crop!"

"Well, let's hope I can save it. In the meantime, only a few more days in the chair, and I can start getting on my feet more and more. I'll be out of everyone's hair in no time."

The sleigh glided along a winding forest path,

pulled by two chestnut horses with bells on their harnesses. Kristen and Mason sat close together on one side of the sleigh, holding hands inside their thick mittens. Ginger noticed Julie and Nolan, the couple in front steering the sleigh, were also holding hands and gazing affectionately at each other. Would she ever find that kind of easy affection and partnership these couples had?

Ginger felt a pang in her chest as she thought of Ethan. Even after their almost kiss while decorating the tree, he had pulled away and distanced himself again.

Kristen sighed contentedly, leaning against Mason's shoulder. "Isn't this romantic?" she asked Ginger. "Just like a Hallmark Christmas movie!"

Ginger smiled. "It certainly is picturesque. And you two seem perfectly happy together."

"We are," Mason said, lifting Kristen's mittened hand to kiss it.

Kristen blushed. "I hope we have more outings together after..." Kristen began then hesitated. "After you've recovered and the holidays are over."

"I'd like that," Ginger said. "If I stick around, that is."

Mason glanced back at Ginger with a knowing smile. "Something tells me you will."

Kristen elbowed him playfully. "Don't get ahead of yourself, matchmaker!" She turned to Ginger. "But really, I do hope you'll stay. We'd love to have you, and I have a feeling Ethan would come around too..."

Ginger's heart leapt at the mention of Ethan's name. "We'll see," she said, hoping her reddening cheeks weren't noticeable. She gazed out at the snowy woods. She was confused by her feelings toward Ethan, but her troubled thoughts were distracted by the jingle of sleigh bells and laughter between old friends sharing a perfect Christmas moment together.

After the ride finished, a few people approached Kristen with worried looks. "We went to Woodward Farm to pick out our tree today," one woman said, "but you didn't have any balsam firs left. Are you getting more in stock?"

Kristen glanced at Ginger, who suddenly felt ill with nerves. The serum. If it didn't work...

Kristen forced a bright smile. "Not to worry, we have more balsams coming soon! There was just a, er, delay in getting them on the lot. Check back tomorrow."

Ginger cast a worried glance at Kristen.

"Don't worry," Kristen said, noticing Ginger's frown. "I'm sure the serum is working and the balsams will be good as new."

"But what if it's not?" Ginger asked. "So much depends on those trees for your family's farm and tradition. If I've failed—"

Just then, Mayor Thompson strode up, tipping his hat. "Why, Dr. Sanders! Lovely to see you up and about. I trust you're finding our little town accommodating during your recovery?"

"Yes, thank you, Mayor Thompson," Ginger said politely, though inwardly, she cringed. She disliked his veiled reminder that her stay here was temporary.

"Glad to hear it!" the mayor said. "Say, I wanted to ask about that special balsam fir you mentioned. I'd love to get a look at that tree."

Kristen and Mason tensed, avoiding each other's gaze. There was no special balsam fir.

But Ginger smiled. "How wonderful! That particular tree is being saved for you, Mayor Thompson. We'll let you know more on Friday."

"Splendid!" The mayor tipped his hat again. "You folks have a lovely day. And do give my regards to young Ethan!" He strode off, whistling a carol.

As soon as he was out of earshot, Kristen smacked Ginger's arm. "Are you crazy?" she whispered. "Promising him a tree we don't even have?"

Ginger winced. "I panicked. I'm sorry! But don't worry... I have an idea."

CHAPTER 20

Ethan sat in the living room, petting George, who sat in his lap. "What a mess this is, George." He sighed. "If we can't fix those balsam firs..."

Just then, Kristen burst through the door with Mason, snowflakes melting in their hair. They were both grinning, eyes bright. Dorothy came out from the kitchen, carrying a tray of frosted sugar cookies and mugs of hot cocoa.

"Cookies and cocoa, anyone?" Dorothy asked.

Ethan took a snowman cookie and bit off its head, thinking his mother seemed determined to fatten them up for winter.

"Where have you two been off to?" Ethan asked between bites of cookie.

"We took Ginger for a sleigh ride!" Kristen said. She gazed up at Mason adoringly, and Ethan felt a pang of longing for the kind of partnership his sister had found.

"It's good to see Ginger out enjoying the town, even with her broken leg," Dorothy said, handing Ethan a mug. "No sense cooping her up in that little cabin! A sleigh ride was perfect."

"The doctor says she can start using crutches for a few hours soon," Kristen said. "So maybe you can have your place back again, Ethan!"

Internally, Ethan thought he'd be glad to escape the farmhouse and go back to his cabin. But the idea of Ginger moving out gave him a strange sense of loss he didn't want to examine too closely.

"You should join them next time, Ethan," his mother said, handing him a mug of cocoa. "Some fresh air would do you good."

Ethan frowned at the thought of being a third wheel, though escaping the farm troubles did sound tempting.

The phone rang, and Ethan answered to hear his friend's grim tone. "Ethan, how're things over there? I heard you've had some... issues with your trees this year?"

"Just a little glitch. Nothing we can't handle,"

Ethan said, hoping he sounded more confident than he felt.

"Well, the mayor's been asking after your balsams," his friend said. "I can't stand the guy, so I've been putting him off. But, Ethan... is everything really all right?"

"Don't worry. We have it under control," Ethan assured him. "I'll let you know if that changes."

After hanging up, he noticed Kristen and Mason's smiles had faded. "What is it?"

Kristen winced. "We ran into the mayor in town, and he asked about that 'special' balsam fir Ginger mentioned..." Kristen told him about Ginger promising the mayor their best balsam fir.

Ethan rubbed his forehead, feeling a stress headache coming on. Though part of him wanted to groan at Ginger's quick promise, he knew Kristen was right—the mayor had put her on the spot. And really, what else could she have said?

"Ginger made a concoction that we hope will fix things, and we applied it last night," Ethan said. "I guess now we'll see if it worked."

"I sure hope so," Kristen said. "For Ginger's sake."

"Be optimistic!" Dorothy said. "Things have a way of working themselves out."

Ethan nodded, hoping his mother was right. The

future of their farm rested on those balsams making a turnaround.

"I'll go check on the trees now," Ethan said, pulling on his boots and grabbing two more cookies for the road.

As Ethan headed out the door, crunching a snowflake cookie, an ominous feeling settled in his gut. He could only hope Ginger's solution had been as magical as she'd envisioned, and that those balsams would recover in time. If not, hard times were surely ahead.

CHAPTER 21

Ginger gazed out the cabin window, waiting anxiously for Ethan to return. When she saw him trudging through the snow toward the cabin, her heart sank. He wasn't smiling.

She let him in, and he held out some balsam branches to her as he stomped the snow off his boots. "I brought these so you could see for yourself."

Ginger inspected the branches, frowning. The needles did look slightly brighter, but beyond that, she saw gray spots and scaly patches on the bark that shouldn't be there. Her heart twisted with worry as she gently ran her fingers over the dying branches.

"Did you notice this on any of the other trees?" She pointed to the scaly patch. "How many trees were affected? Did you see more of these gray spots? And the bark—were there patches that looked split?"

Ethan peered at the branch. "I… I didn't notice any of that."

He seemed down on himself, so Ginger put her hand on his arm. "It's okay. You wouldn't have noticed. I'm trained to because this is a sign of fungal disease."

"Oh no." Ethan looked into her eyes, and she felt a jolt. It was as if she could see clear into his soul and feel how upset he was. The sadness in his sapphire eyes nearly broke her heart.

"Don't worry. I can fix this. And look…" She pointed to the needles. "The fertilizer concoction seems to be working. Now I just need to figure out the right treatment for the fungus. But if only I could get out there and see for myself."

They gazed out at the winter landscape.

"There's no way I can make it out there with this leg," Ginger said.

"It seems like we're so close…" Ethan said, his voice trailing off.

"But I opened my big mouth and promised the mayor a tree by Friday."

Ethan turned from the window and looked at her. "It's not your fault. You did the right thing. Bought us some time, anyway."

"If only I could see the damage myself. Seeing a bigger sample would give me a better idea, but if I could just get a proper look..."

Ethan gazed at the snowy ground and shook his head. "I don't see how. You'll just hurt yourself worse if you try trekking through this mess."

"It sure is messy. The only time I've been out is when I went to the doctor and the sleigh ride," Ginger said.

Ethan's face suddenly lit up. "The sled! I can bundle you up and pull you out there myself. Not as good as a sleigh ride, but it could do the trick. You might be able to get close enough, if we're real careful."

Ginger's eyes shone with renewed hope. "That's perfect! As long as we're careful, I should be able to make it. At least I might get close enough to make a better diagnosis and figure out a plan."

Ethan grinned, opening the hall closet and grabbing extra blankets. "All right, let's get you loaded up! The trees need you, and it'll be good for you to get some fresh air. Just promise you'll tell me if you start hurting—your health comes before anything else."

"It's a deal." Ginger's heart warmed at his concern, and she was excited about getting outside and being able to inspect the trees. And something else too—the sense of teamwork and camaraderie between her and Ethan was exhilarating. Judging by the way he had suddenly shed his grumpy demeanor, she suspected Ethan might feel the same way.

❄

ETHAN HELPED Ginger into the sled, tucking blankets snugly around her. She was wearing a pink knit hat, and snowflakes clung to her long eyelashes. Her cheeks were flushed from the cold, making her look radiant. His heart did an odd little flip at how cute she looked bundled up for their mission.

As Ethan pulled the sled through the snow, Ginger stretched out a mittened hand to catch drifting flakes. "This is the most fun I've had in ages!" she said. "I love being outside, don't you?"

Ethan grinned. "I sure do."

As Ethan pulled Ginger through the snowy woods, their conversation flowed as easily as if they were old friends.

"Smell that pine," Ginger said, inhaling deeply. "Nothing quite like it."

"Reminds me of being a kid," Ethan said, "climbing trees and getting sticky with sap."

Ginger laughed. "Like when we first shook hands?"

Ethan smiled at the memory. "Yep. It wasn't so bad."

"I was the same as a kid. Mom always had a fit when I came home covered in sap and leaves."

Ethan grinned at the image of a young, feisty Ginger shimmying up the pine trees.

Ginger sighed. "It's so quiet and peaceful out here. You're so lucky to have this. I'd much rather be out here than in the city crowded with people."

"I totally agree." Ethan's heart swelled at the connection. He much preferred the woods with its trees, birds, and animals to people.

When they reached the edge of the grove, Ginger peered out from her nest of blankets and pointed to a towering balsam fir. "There. That's the first one I need to see up close."

Ethan pulled the sled right up to its sweeping branches. Ginger tugged off her mitten and reached out to gently turn the needles and inspect the bark, brow furrowed in concern. Ethan kept a steadying hand on her back, struck by her tenderness in handling the branches.

"This little guy took a hard hit," Ginger said, "but I think we caught it just in time. See, here's where the fungus started spreading, but it hasn't penetrated too deep yet." Her eyes shone with purpose. "With the right treatment, we'll have this one good as new in no time."

Ginger instructed him to move to the next gate, and he pulled her over, stopping so she could diagnose the damage. "This one is not bad either."

As they continued on, Ginger pointed out trees she wanted to inspect. Ethan pulled her over, supported her when she tried to stand in the snow, and handed her clippers when she wanted to cut off a branch. Their teamwork felt natural.

"This fungus is sneaky," Ginger said, peering at an afflicted balsam. "But it hasn't taken hold yet. And not every tree is affected. If the solution you applied yesterday does its job, you'll be able to cut some trees for the tree lot on Thursday, and that tall one over there will be ready for the mayor to inspect."

As they headed back, Ginger gazed up through the branches, eyes lighting up. "Look, a perfect opening to see the stars! Can we pause for a bit?"

Ethan gladly pulled the sled into a clearing. Did Ginger love stargazing too? It was one of his favorite things. She slid over and motioned for him to sit next to her.

They tilted their heads back, taking in the blanket of inky sky stretched above.

"Look! There's the Big Dipper!" Ginger pointed.

"And Cassiopeia to the west," Ethan added.

"I didn't realize you were a stargazer," Ginger said.

"Oh sure, living out here in the country. But you're from the city. Can't be too many opportunities to look at stars with all those city lights."

"That's for sure. I actually miss being able to do that. The city isn't all it's cracked up to be."

Ginger sounded regretful, and Ethan looked at her. With her eyes tipped up to the sky and the look of joy on her face, he realized how beautiful she was. "You mean you don't want to live there anymore?" Why did that thought make him feel so hopeful?

Ginger turned to look at him. Their eyes met, and he felt a sizzle of connection.

She looked back up at the sky. "Maybe not. I grew up in the country. We had a big field in the backyard, perfect for stargazing. Sometimes I think it would be nice to go back to my roots. My dad taught me the constellations."

"Mine too," Ethan said, returning his gaze to the constellations. Memories of sitting out here with his father bubbled up.

Ethan nodded, the weight of her question hanging in the cool air between them. "Yes. That's why everything feels so overwhelming now. With the trees, the farm... It's all resting on my shoulders." His voice wavered slightly, a testament to his inner turmoil.

Ginger reached over, slipping her hand into his. The warmth of her touch seeped into his cold fingers, her grip firm and comforting. "Don't worry, Ethan," she said with conviction. "We're going to revive the trees. Everything will work out. I know it will."

For some reason, Ethan found himself believing in her words. Her confidence ignited a glimmer of hope within him. For the first time in what seemed like an eternity, he felt a sense of peace coursing through him. With a start, he realized he'd totally forgotten to act grumpy.

As he looked at Ginger, her face illuminated by the starlight, he realized he didn't want to hide behind that gruff façade anymore. Perhaps, he thought, it was time to let someone in. He had used his grinch exterior as a shield, pushing people away, but now it seemed less necessary. Maybe it was time for a change.

❄

GINGER'S MIND swirled with possibilities as she breathed in the night air. Out here, embraced by open spaces, unmarred by traffic, she felt a renewed connection to nature. The sweet, crisp scent of pine hung in the air, stirring a deep fondness for rural life within her. She wondered, could this tranquil town of Pinecone Falls have a place for someone like her?

She snuck a glance at Ethan. She was mesmerized by the way the moonlight illuminated his features. The hard lines around his eyes seemed to fade away as he spoke, revealing a glimpse of the carefree young man he must have been.

She'd noticed that he'd lost his gruff demeanor. She had suspected he had a softer side, and she was right. But she could tell he'd been hurt. She'd seen the look in his eye when they were putting up the tree and heard it in his voice when he'd talked about his father.

It made her even more determined to make sure that these trees got better soon.

Ethan glanced over at her, a soft smile playing on his lips. "It's beautiful here, isn't it? I feel lucky every day to live in a place like this."

His words echoed her own thoughts. "It really is," she said. "The scenery, the community—everything about Pinecone Falls seems perfect. I can see why you never wanted to leave."

"We have a simple life here, but it's good," he said. "Family, nature, tradition—those are the things that really matter."

Ginger's heart swelled at his words. After years of

wandering, it was a life she craved for herself. A place to put down roots, a community to belong to, and maybe even a family of her own someday.

She shook off the thought, blaming the chill for her fanciful notions. But she couldn't deny the connection she felt with Ethan in that moment, as if their souls had recognized each other from some other life.

The cold seeped into Ginger's bones, causing her to shiver. She wrapped her arms around herself, rubbing her hands up and down her sleeves to generate warmth.

Ethan glanced over in concern. "Are you cold? We should probably head back soon."

"Just a bit," she said, teeth chattering. "I didn't realize how much the temperature would drop."

Without another word, Ethan shrugged out of his jacket and draped it over her shoulders. The lingering warmth enveloped her instantly, along with the earthy, woodsy scent of him.

She sighed in contentment, snuggling into the soft flannel. "Thank you. You didn't have to do that."

"Can't have you turning into an ice cube," he said gruffly. "Ma would never forgive me if I let that happen."

Ginger smiled, wondering if his concern stemmed

from more than just his mother's wrath. She found she didn't mind either way. Having his jacket wrapped around her and his solid presence beside her was comforting in a way she hadn't felt since she was a little girl.

Maybe this was what coming home felt like.

"We should probably head back," Ethan said.

Ginger started to protest, not wanting the night to end. But her teeth were beginning to chatter, and Ethan didn't even have a coat, so he must have been even colder than her.

"I think that's a good idea," she said reluctantly. As Ethan helped her into the sled, she took one last look at the starry sky. She had a feeling that this night, and this place, would stay with her for a long time to come.

CHAPTER 22

When they got back to the cabin, Ginger invited Ethan in to eat the food he'd brought over in the basket earlier. He could hardly refuse—he was starving, and he didn't want his time with Ginger to end.

The mouthwatering aroma of the chicken pot pie filled the air as they warmed it up together.

"You know," Ethan said, trying to maneuver around Ginger's wheelchair, "I never thought my kitchen would feel so small. And with the kittens, it's like an obstacle course in here."

Ginger laughed as she watched one of the kittens attempt to leap onto the counter, only to slide back down the cabinets, its claws making a scraping noise on the wooden surface. "Well, you could always consider it a team-building exercise," she teased.

As they continued cooking, the kittens weaved between their legs, purring and occasionally pawing at their pants legs. The scents of cooking food and the occasional meow from the kittens created a warm and homey atmosphere.

Ethan grinned as he watched Ginger expertly chop some fresh herbs to sprinkle on the pot pie. "You're a natural in the kitchen, even with all the chaos," he complimented her. "And you seem to have a way with these kittens too."

Ginger smiled as one of the kittens climbed onto her lap and kneaded her thigh with its tiny paws. "Well, I've always loved animals, and it seems these little ones have taken a liking to me as well. I could never have a pet as a kid but always wanted one."

Ethan's heart pinched. He thought that was incredibly sad; he'd always had a pet as a kid.

As they waited for the pot pie to finish baking, the kittens continued to explore the kitchen, occasionally finding themselves in precarious situations. One of them attempted to climb the curtains, while another managed to paw open a cabinet door, only to be gently nudged back out by Ethan.

Ethan watched Ginger expertly navigate the tight

space of the kitchen in her wheelchair, and he couldn't help but comment, "You've adapted pretty well to that wheelchair, but I know it can't be easy."

Ginger smiled, her eyes meeting Ethan's. "Thanks. Actually, the doctor said I might be able to fully transition to crutches in a few more days. I've been practicing a bit when I have some privacy." She looked at him with a hint of excitement. "Want to see?"

"Sure," Ethan said, curiosity piqued.

Ginger grabbed the crutches that were leaning against the wall nearby and positioned them under her arms. She rose slowly, balancing herself with the crutches as she took a few cautious steps. Ethan watched in admiration, impressed by her determination.

However, just as Ginger was starting to gain confidence, the three kittens darted underfoot, causing her to lose her balance. Ethan instinctively reached out and caught her just before she hit the floor, their faces suddenly inches apart.

For a moment, their eyes locked, and Ethan felt a surge of emotion that made him want to lean in and kiss her. But before he could act on the impulse, the kittens playfully leaped onto his legs, meowing and vying for his attention.

Ethan chuckled and let out a breath he didn't

realize he'd been holding. "I guess we have our own little feline security detail, huh?" He helped Ginger back onto her feet and steadied her with the crutches.

Ginger laughed, her cheeks flushed from the near fall and the momentary tension between them. "Seems like it. They certainly know how to keep things interesting."

As they returned their attention to the kittens, Ethan felt a sense of relief that the moment had passed, unsure of what the consequences might have been. Still, there was a lingering curiosity about what could have happened if the kittens hadn't interrupted them.

Ethan, rattled from the almost kiss, picked up the kittens and began to coo and pet them, his face softening as they curled up in his arms.

"Aha!" Ginger exclaimed with a knowing smile. "I knew you were really an animal lover."

Ethan shrugged it off, trying to act nonchalant. "Who can't love kittens?" He gently set them down, and they immediately started to play at his feet.

Ginger's smile turned wistful. "I'm going to miss them when Myrtle comes to get them in a few days."

Ethan paused, realizing that not only would the kittens be leaving, but Ginger would be too. The cabin would feel empty and lifeless without their presence. He shook off the feeling and focused on their dinner.

As they ate, the twinkling lights on the tree cast a warm glow over the room, snow fell gently outside, and the purring kittens snuggled close. The atmosphere was perfect, and the conversation turned to Ginger's plan for the trees.

"So, I've been mulling this over," Ginger began, her voice charged with enthusiasm. "The trees need to be healthy again in just a few days. I've got a plan, but there are three different ways to approach it, and I'm not sure which is faster. If we work together, we can speed things up, and I'm pretty sure we'll have good trees to sell in the lot and the tree the mayor wants for the lighting in no time."

Ethan raised an eyebrow, intrigued by her confidence. "You've really thought this through, haven't you?"

Ginger flashed him a mischievous grin. "Well, I do have a PhD in tree-saving, you know." She chuckled at her own joke then continued. "The first approach involves treating each tree individually, which is time-consuming. The second is a more general treatment for the whole area, but it might not be as effective. And the third is a combination of the two."

Ethan considered the options, his expression

thoughtful. "Sounds like we've got our work cut out for us. But I'm game. We can tackle this together."

As they discussed the pros and cons of each approach, the camaraderie between them grew stronger. Their passion for the trees fueled their determination, and as they brainstormed together, Ethan felt optimistic about the trees.

But another transformation was taking shape, one that both excited him and filled him with trepidation. As they talked, he felt a strong tug, a connection blossoming between them. For the first time since Sarah's death, he wondered if maybe he could find love again.

CHAPTER 23

The morning sun filtered through the curtains, casting a warm glow on the wooden floor of the farmhouse. Ethan awoke feeling a renewed sense of purpose, eager to start the day and execute the plan he and Ginger had devised the night before. He got up, stretched, and headed to the kitchen, where his mother and his sister were already enjoying their morning coffee.

George sauntered into the room, rubbing against Ethan's legs as he poured himself a cup of coffee. The rich aroma filled the air, and Ethan took a sip, feeling the warmth spread through him.

"So, how are things going with the trees?" Kristen asked, concern etched into her face.

Ethan reassured them with a confident smile.

"Ginger and I have come up with a plan. We're going to work together to make sure we get balsam firs on the lot as soon as possible and we have one for the mayor to look at."

Dorothy raised an eyebrow, a mischievous glint in her eye. "You two have been spending quite a bit of time together lately, haven't you?"

Ethan felt a blush creeping up his cheeks but tried to brush off her insinuation. "Well, we're just working on the trees. She's a real expert, you know."

Kristen smirked, giving Ethan a knowing look. "Whatever you say, Ethan. But it's nice to see you working with someone who shares your passion for the farm."

Ethan agreed. As he finished his coffee, he thought about the tasks ahead and how much he was looking forward to working alongside Ginger. Speaking of which, he'd better get going on gathering the supplies they needed.

He checked the list they'd made the night before. There were several ingredients Ginger needed for the new serum she was working on, which would help fight the fungus on the trees. One of the crucial ingredients was a natural antifungal agent called neem oil.

"Hey, do either of you know where I can find neem oil? Ginger needs it for the serum she's working on."

Kristen raised an eyebrow, intrigued. "Neem oil? I think we might have some in the shed near the farmhouse. I remember using it a couple of years ago for a gardening project."

Dorothy nodded in agreement. "Yes, I believe that's where we keep it. Check the shelves near the back."

Ethan thanked them and headed to the shed, the crisp morning air invigorating him as he walked. He rummaged through the shelves and finally found the bottle of neem oil tucked away behind some gardening tools. He also found a spray bottle, which was one of the other things Ginger had asked for. With the essential ingredient in hand, he set off toward the cabin, eager to deliver it to Ginger so she could continue her work on the serum.

Ginger was already hard at work, with pots boiling on the stove. The air was filled with the scents of various herbal concoctions. The three kittens were playing near Ginger's wheelchair, and Ethan picked two of them up and began to pet them.

"I'm getting really attached to these little furballs," Ginger admitted, a soft, affectionate look in her eyes.

Ethan put the kittens down, realizing that he felt the same. That wasn't good. He couldn't keep them. Could he?

He pulled the oil bottle out of his jacket pocket. "Here's the neem oil you needed."

"Thank you." Ginger took the bottle and scrutinized the label. "I've been working on a new formula for the serum, and I've added an accelerant to it. It should help dry up the fungus more quickly. We'll need to spray the trees in a specific way to ensure the solution reaches the affected areas."

"I got a sprayer too. It's in the truck."

Ginger nodded as she measured out a few drops of the pungent neem oil, wrinkling her nose at the bitterness clinging to her fingers. "Just a few drops of this should do to boost the antifungal properties."

Ethan peered over her shoulder into the vial, skeptical. "A few drops? Are you sure that will be enough?"

Ginger arched an eyebrow. "This stuff is strong. Not all problems are solved through excess," Ginger replied. "Sometimes a delicate hand is best."

Ethan's eyes gleamed with humor. "Is that what you call your measures so far? Delicate?" He gestured at the counters overflowing with vials and beakers bubbling and steaming.

Ginger pursed her lips, struggling not to smile. "This is nothing. You should see how my lab looks. Now step aside before your enthusiasm for 'just a bit more' undoes all my careful work."

Ethan laughed and raised his hands in mock defeat, conceding her point. In truth, her exacting standards were what most gave him hope.

Ginger shook one of the beakers, and the amber serum swirled inside. "This is done. Let's get it into the sprayer."

Ethan got the sprayer from the truck, and Ginger poured the solution in then instructed him on how to properly spray the trees, emphasizing the importance of thorough coverage. "We'll check back in the evening to see how the trees are responding. If all goes well, we should see some noticeable improvements."

❄

GINGER WATCHED as Ethan ventured into the snow-covered grove of trees, carrying the serum and the sprayer. She silently crossed her fingers, hoping everything would go smoothly. As he disappeared into the wintry landscape, she scooped up one of the kittens and cuddled it close, feeling its soft purr vibrate against her chest.

The cabin looked festive with the little tree. Yet she realized something was missing—the cabin didn't have that nostalgic scent of fresh pine boughs she associated with the season.

Ginger dialed Mason's number and waited for him to pick up. When he answered, she couldn't help but let excitement color her voice. "Hey, Mason, I have a favor to ask. Would you and Kristen be able to take me to the Woodward tree lot to pick up some pine boughs? I think it would really make the cabin smell more like Christmas."

Mason hesitated for a moment before responding, "Are you sure you'll be up for that? I don't know if your wheelchair will do well on the lot. It's snowy."

Ginger reassured him, "I can use my crutches. The doctor said I need to spend a few hours each day on them anyway, so I thought I'd use those hours for something fun."

Mason hesitated for a second before answering. "Okay. I know how you are when you get your mind set to something. How about we swing by in two hours? That should give you some time to prepare."

"Perfect," Ginger replied, her spirits lifted. "I'll be ready. Thanks, Mason. I really appreciate it."

With a plan in place, Ginger set about tidying up the cabin, clearing away any clutter from their earlier activities. She washed the pots and pans, wiped down the countertops, and cleared off some space on the mantel and table for pine boughs.

CHAPTER 24

The air in the tree lot was pungent with the scent of fresh pine. Ginger was getting used to her crutches and managed to hobble along without tripping. Kristen and Mason hovered on either side of her, ready to keep her from face-planting, but luckily her usual clumsiness didn't surface.

She passed dozens of customers choosing trees from the rows of firs. Ginger hobbled over to a nearby pile of pine boughs, her crutches clacking against the ground.

"This one's perfect." Ginger reached out to grab a few boughs. She put them to her nose and inhaled deeply. "Holiday heaven!"

But as she leaned on her crutches, one of them slipped out from under her. She let out a yelp as she stumbled, almost falling over. Mason and Kristen both reacted quickly, each grabbing an arm to steady her. Ginger flushed with embarrassment but laughed it off.

"I guess I'm still getting the hang of these crutches," she admitted, feeling grateful for their quick reflexes.

"No worries, Ginger. We've got your back," Mason reassured her, his tone light and supportive.

"Thanks. You always do." Ginger smiled fondly at her friend. "But I hope I get used to these things soon. I feel like I might be overstaying my welcome at Ethan's cabin."

Kristen waved off her concerns with a dismissive hand. "Nonsense! Ethan doesn't mind at all. You're helping us, after all. Besides, I think he enjoys the company at the farmhouse."

Ginger chuckled. "Maybe you're right."

"Speaking of which," Ginger continued, her voice dropping to a conspiratorial whisper, "Ethan is out with the new serum now."

Before she could finish, an exasperated voice from the other side of the trees interrupted their conversation.

"I can't believe the balsams are not out yet," one woman said, frustration dripping from her words.

"I know. It's such a disappointment," another added, her tone equally disheartened.

Ginger exchanged a concerned glance with Mason and Kristen. They needed to make the treatment work not just for the farm, but for the people of Pinecone Falls who cherished their Christmas traditions.

Ginger turned as a familiar voice reached her ears. "Dr. Sanders, a pleasure to see you. I hope your leg is improving."

Mayor Thompson stood behind her, a cordial smile on his face. Ginger noted the intense gleam in his eyes that betrayed his friendly demeanor.

"My leg?" Ginger lifted her crutches slightly, returning his smile with a bit of strain. "Improving. I'll be back to normal soon, thanks to these crutches."

"And the trees?" His voice was almost casual, but the slight stiffening of his posture revealed his concern.

Just as Ginger was about to reply, Mayor Thompson interrupted. "You see, Dr. Sanders, it's imperative that we have the tree in the town square by Saturday. I had hoped to select one from the Woodward farm. You stated one would be ready, but with no report on where and when I could see it, I have made arrangements with Shady Pines Tree Farm from the next town over."

A rush of panic washed over Ginger. She couldn't let that happen. She'd worked tirelessly to save the Woodward trees. They meant so much to the Woodward family, and Ethan...

Ginger blurted out a response, her voice steady despite the inner turmoil. "Actually, Mayor, there's no need to worry. We've been prepping the trees. They'll not only look good but last longer too." The words flowed smoothly. Her lie was so convincingly delivered that she herself almost believed it. "Why don't you drop by tonight to see for yourself?"

Mayor Thompson blinked, obviously taken aback. "Tonight, you say? After supper?"

"That would be perfect." Ginger fought to keep her smile in place as he nodded and excused himself.

As he retreated, Kristen tugged at her sleeve. "Ginger, is that true? The trees will be ready?"

Inhaling deeply, Ginger crossed her fingers behind her back. "Ethan applied the latest treatment this morning. Let's just hope it worked."

CHAPTER 25

With the afternoon sunshine bouncing off the frosted ground, Ethan sauntered down the main street of Pinecone Falls. Was it his imagination, or did the lights seem brighter and the decorations more vibrant? As he breathed in the crisp air, Ethan couldn't help but feel the infectious holiday cheer that he had overlooked before.

Passing the Moosehead, a popular local pub, Ethan caught sight of his friends through the frost-kissed windows. Recognizing the familiar figures of burly Brad, bespectacled Will, and ever-chatty Mike, he decided to pop in for a bite. The scent of roasting chestnuts and hearty stew was already wafting out, and his stomach gave an approving grumble.

His friends beckoned him over, their surprised

grins stretching across their faces as he slid into the booth beside them. The clink of their beer mugs in greeting echoed in the bustling pub.

Soon, Jake, their favorite waiter, scurried over. A young man with round glasses and a mop of curly dark hair, he expertly balanced a tray holding mugs of foamy beer. He passed out the beer and took their lunch orders.

Ethan's gaze traveled over his friends—Brad, Will and Mike—three individuals as different as they were tight-knit. He hadn't realized how much he'd missed these casual, carefree moments until now.

Will, the practical one of the group, was the first to speak up. "You've been a hermit lately," he said, his tone teasing but with a hint of genuine concern. "It's good to see you out and about."

Ethan rubbed the back of his neck, a sudden rush of guilt washing over him. He'd been holed up in his cabin for so long, consumed by his grief, and had unintentionally left his friends in the lurch.

"Yeah, I guess I've been a bit of a recluse. My apologies, guys," Ethan confessed, looking around the table, meeting each of their understanding gazes.

Mike, the joker, lightened the moment, as he always did. He clapped Ethan on the back, nearly sending him into his plate of fries. "Bit of a hermit?

Mate, you make a mountain man look like a social butterfly!"

His joviality broke the tension, and the table erupted in laughter. Ethan couldn't help but join in, grateful for the levity.

Their laughter subsided, and Brad, the quiet and thoughtful one, chimed in. "It's good to have you back, Ethan. We've missed you." His words were simple, yet they carried a weight that made Ethan's chest tighten.

They'd missed him. Despite his self-imposed exile, his friends had missed him. Ethan's eyes misted over slightly, and he nodded, struggling to voice his gratitude. His friends, these three men he'd known for years, hadn't just written him off. They hadn't pressured him, hadn't forced him to move on before he was ready. Instead, they had quietly supported him from the sidelines.

He took a deep breath and managed a sincere "Thanks, guys."

Mike, ever the instigator, leaned back in his chair, a mischievous twinkle in his eyes. "Does this change of mood have anything to do with that cute redhead I've been seeing at your place?" he asked, nudging Ethan playfully with his elbow.

The table fell into a knowing silence, three pairs of eyes all focused on Ethan.

Ethan choked on his beer, coughing a bit, before he managed to regain his composure. "She's helping with the farm, not living with me. I moved into the farmhouse with Mom and Kristen," he said, feeling his cheeks heat up. But the insinuation had already been made, and he saw his friends exchanging amused glances.

Ethan couldn't help the sudden rush of warmth he felt at Mike's comment. It wasn't unwelcome, just unexpected.

A flash of memory washed over him—Ginger wrapped up in a blanket by the fireplace, the kittens curled up in her lap, and the glow from the Christmas tree lights reflecting in her eyes. It was an image of domesticity that felt too comforting, too inviting.

Ethan realized with a jolt that he hadn't thought about Sarah for a few days. For once, he wasn't overwhelmed with guilt. Instead, he was filled with a warm sense of acceptance. Things were changing, he was changing, and for the first time in a long while, he felt at peace with it.

❄

ETHAN EMERGED FROM THE PUB, a buoyancy to his step that hadn't been there before. A newfound lightness filled him, as if a weight had been lifted. The pub's door swung closed behind him, leaving him with the hum of midday traffic and the crisp winter air.

His old truck rumbled to life, and he found himself steering it, almost instinctively, toward the iron-gated cemetery.

As he cruised along the path leading toward Sarah's grave, the tall pine tree standing guard nearby became visible. The tree, stark against the snow-covered cemetery, always seemed to hold a gentle reverence for the stone it sheltered. He pulled his truck over, the gravel crunching under the tires, and stepped out.

Usually, he felt filled with sorrow and guilt when he came here. But today, it was different. The cloak of sadness that usually draped over him seemed to have been shed. His guilt was strangely silent.

With a respectful nod to the carved stone, he stepped forward and ran his fingers over the cold granite. Its icy touch was no longer a grim reminder, but a solid testament to a love that once was.

Then something unusual happened. The cardinal, a vibrant spot of red against the winter white, usually a silent observer from the pine tree, fluttered down and perched on the top of the gravestone.

He watched it in surprise. "What's this now?"

It looked at him, chirped a melodious note that sounded remarkably like approval, and then took off into the blue. As it disappeared into the distance, Ethan felt an unexplained lightness fill his heart. It was as if the cardinal had carried away the last remnants of his guilt, giving him silent permission to move forward. It was an almost absurd thought, but he couldn't help but think it was Sarah, sending him a message. A message that reassured him, in the oddest way, that everything was going to be okay.

As he stepped back into his truck, hope welled up inside him. His heart felt lighter, his mind clearer. The image of Ginger, her fiery hair dancing in the night breeze as they'd talked beneath the star-kissed sky, began to bloom in his mind.

Before, guilt had kept his budding feelings for Ginger firmly in check. It felt too disloyal to Sarah to even think about another relationship. But now, it felt like the wall had lowered. But he had bigger problems. Making sure the trees were healthy was his first priority. His personal life would have to wait.

His tires crunched on the frozen ground as he arrived at the tree farm. The winter air carried the rustic scent of the woodland to his nose. He drove with a mission, making a beeline toward the balsams. If there was any progress with them, it would be an emblem of hope, not just for the farm, but for him personally.

Leaving his truck behind, he trudged through the snow. The cold seeping through his boots failed to dampen his optimism. The trees around him stood in regimented lines. A flock of birds took flight, their wings cutting through the silent air.

But as he reached the balsams, his heart clenched. His hand reached out, fingers running over the browning needles that fell off at his touch. He looked closer to see fresh green needles sprouting. That was a good sign, but the bark still bore the mottled signs of the fungus. It seemed like it wasn't as bad as before, though. Or was that just his imagination? He moved from tree to tree, each one mirroring the disappointment of the last.

A sigh escaped his lips, melting into the winter air. His heart, which had been on the rise, sank like a stone. The remedy hadn't fully worked.

CHAPTER 26

Ginger stood at the cabin window, clutching the smallest kitten, which she'd named Geraldine, against her chest. She'd already thought up names for all three and was probably getting too attached. It wasn't just the kittens she was getting too attached to. It was this cabin, the town, and the Woodwards, especially Ethan.

Her gaze swept across the snowy landscape to where Ethan was emerging from the tree farm. His broad shoulders were slumped, his stride less energetic than when he'd left. She could sense the disappointment rolling off him even from this distance.

As Ginger watched him, she realized how entwined her life had become with this place—Pinecone Falls, the Woodward family, this cozy cabin

—and especially Ethan. It had only been a short time, but what happened with the trees mattered to her.

With a sigh, she redirected her attention to the ball of fluff in her hands. It wasn't just the kittens she was falling for. She was falling for Ethan and everything that came with him. Her mind began weaving dreams of a new life here, working from home in this quaint town.

Maybe moving to Pinecone Falls was just the change she needed. She already worked from home quite a bit, and even though she couldn't just drive into the office at a moment's notice, she was sure her boss wouldn't mind.

But first, they had to fix the trees.

She wheeled over to the door and opened it, letting in a swirl of snow and chilly air as Ethan approached. "How did it go?"

He grimaced and bent down to scoop up one of the other kittens—Gabriella—who had tried to escape out the door. "Fungus… still there," he admitted, his voice hoarse.

"And the needles?" Ginger pressed, her heart sinking at his downcast expression.

"There's some new green," he offered, but she could see the hopelessness in his eyes. "I don't think these trees are going to be ready. I feel like I'm failing my family and, worst of all, my father."

She reached out, her hand landing softly on his arm. "Ethan," she said, her voice filled with conviction, "he'd be proud of the way you are facing this challenge. The important thing is not to give up. I'm sure I can find something else to try."

"I need to find a way to stall the mayor," Ethan said, his voice tense.

Ginger felt a twist of unease in her stomach. "Oh, umm... about the mayor..."

Ethan set Gabriella down and frowned at Ginger. "What about him?"

Ginger bit her lip, fidgeting with a loose thread on her sweater. "Well, I ran into him at the tree lot when I was gathering pine boughs for the cabin," she confessed, glancing toward the festively adorned mantel. "And he was... well, quite brusque. He mentioned the possibility of going to another tree farm!"

Ginger could see Ethan's shock and immediately regretted not saying something sooner. "So, I might have... umm... sort of told him we had a tree ready for his inspection tonight," she admitted sheepishly.

Ethan blinked at her in disbelief. "You told him what? Why?"

She shrugged, her cheeks burning with embarrassment. “I don’t know… wishful thinking?”

Ethan sighed and ran a hand through his tousled hair. “All right, well… Let’s see what we can do about this.” He took a deep breath as if steeling himself for the task ahead. “I’ll head to the mayor’s office. Maybe I’ll think up something brilliant on the way that I can use to get him to reschedule coming to see the tree.”

As Ethan marched out of the cabin, leaving a swirl of cold air behind him, Ginger felt guilt gnawing at her. She watched the door close behind him, her mind racing. Had she just ruined everything with her big mouth?

A spark of an idea ignited in her mind. It was a long shot, but it was all she had left. With renewed determination, Ginger opened her hefty botany books, ready to dive in. She might not be able to change what she’d done, but she wasn’t about to give up.

CHAPTER 27

Every corner of Pinecone Falls was bursting with Christmas spirit. Snowmen sporting vibrant scarves waved from yards, fairy lights twinkled like constellations on each tree, and oversized ornaments swung from every porch. The town was the epitome of holiday joy. But Ethan barely registered it.

A single question whirled in his mind: how could he delay the mayor without ruining the Woodward reputation? His grip tightened on the steering wheel. The answer eluded him.

The mayor's office was in a brick building in the center of town. Ethan entered, his boots echoing on the polished marble tiles.

"Hi, Sheila," he said, managing a smile for the receptionist, a middle-aged woman with a warm smile and glasses perched on her nose. "Is Mayor Thompson in?"

"Ethan Woodward!" Sheila greeted him, her eyes lighting up with familiar warmth. "I've missed seeing your dad around here. It's good to see you stepping up. The mayor's got his hands full today, though. You might be waiting a while."

Ethan nodded, his heart sinking. "No problem, I'll wait." He slumped into a chair, the weight of disappointment settling over him. His gaze fixed on the mayor's closed office door.

As time dragged on, the office's quiet ambiance turned his thoughts introspective. The scent of pine wafting from a wreath on Sheila's desk caught his attention.

"Sheila," Ethan began, peering at the wreath, "is this from our lot?" A fleeting moment of pride flashed within him at the possibility.

"It is." Sheila smiled. "I wouldn't buy anywhere else."

Ethan didn't know if that made him feel better or worse. At least she hadn't mentioned the absence of the balsam firs in the lot. But her words only reminded him that many in town were depending on him to provide them.

Her phone buzzed, and she picked it up then shot

Ethan an apologetic look. "I'm sorry, Ethan. The mayor's not going to be able to fit you in. Can you come back tomorrow?"

Defeat squeezed Ethan's heart. "Sure. Thanks, Sheila." He managed a small smile for the receptionist on his way out.

As he trudged down the snow-dusted path, a familiar face hailed him. Ethan recognized the sturdy silhouette of Bob Wainwright standing in front of the Pinecone Falls Café. Bob, with his snowy beard and creased smile lines, was an enduring part of the town's charm. The trusted town doctor had become his father's close friend, always there with wise words and a listening ear.

"Ethan!" Bob's voice echoed across the street, his vibrant blue eyes brightening as he spotted Ethan. "Seems like it's been ages! Care to join an old man for some pie?"

Feeling the weight of his worries, Ethan nodded, welcoming the idea of some friendly chatter. The comforting aromas of cinnamon and freshly brewed coffee greeted them as they stepped into the café.

Over slices of warm apple pie, Ethan found himself confiding in Bob about the challenges he was facing at the farm. Bob listened attentively, nodding occasionally, the compassionate creases around his eyes deepening as Ethan spoke.

Finally, after polishing off his pie, Bob leaned back in his chair, gazing at Ethan thoughtfully. "Your father loved you, Ethan. His pride was never about the Christmas trees, but about who you are. Remember, life is about growth and change. It's high time you embraced it."

Bob's words resonated within Ethan as he made his way back to his truck. He was evolving, allowing the guilt about Sarah to recede, and preparing to step into a new chapter of his life. Perhaps it was time for him to shape the farm in his own way, moving beyond his father's shadow and letting go of the fear of letting people down.

Were the trees really that important? Would it be the end of the world if he couldn't put out balsam firs this year or provide the town with the tree for the Christmas Eve lighting? Probably not. Perhaps he'd had his priorities mixed up, but luckily, it wasn't too late to change them.

He climbed into his truck and started the engine. The soft purr intertwined with his steady heartbeat. As he drove away, the twinkle of the town's Christmas lights in his rearview mirror seemed to echo his sentiments.

His heart fluttered with anticipation as he thought of returning to his cabin and seeing Ginger. The prospect of her company brought a surge of warmth that cut through the winter chill and sparked hope for the future. He smiled, realizing that maybe things weren't so bleak after all.

CHAPTER 28

As Ginger zipped the final suitcase, she felt a pang of sadness. She didn't want to leave, but she'd failed the Woodwards, and she couldn't bear to see the look of disappointment on Ethan's face.

Mason stood in the doorway, his brow furrowed, casting long glances at the precarious luggage tower. "Ginger, are you sure about this? The stairs at the Cozy Holly Inn could be problematic."

She glanced out toward the rows of trees. She'd come up with a last-ditch attempt for the trees, and she'd called Mason and had him use the sled to lug her out so she could apply it. All she could do now was keep her fingers crossed and wait. But if it failed like her past attempts, it was better if she moved back into the inn.

"Yep. The doctor said I can be fully on crutches, and I've inconvenienced the Woodwards enough already." Ginger glanced out toward the rows of trees again.

"Are you sure? You're not exactly graceful, and I know Kristen and Dorothy love having you here." Mason seemed genuinely concerned.

"Not graceful?" Ginger punched him playfully in the arm, the movement almost toppling her over on her crutches. "I'll be fine."

To tell the truth, Ginger wasn't sure how she was going to navigate the stairs at the inn. With her uncoordinated movements, she'd almost taken a few spills on level ground. But she couldn't stay here anymore.

"If you say so." Mason picked up one of the suitcases. "I know how stubborn you are, so I'll just do as you say."

Ginger laughed. "Besides, I could use some advice from the knitting crew over there on my project." Ginger patted the tote bag full of tangled yarn.

A soft patter of paws echoed on the wooden floor, drawing Ginger's gaze to the trio of kittens scampering toward her. Their tiny forms, full of energy and curiosity, blurred into a flurry of orange and white.

Gwendoline, the largest of the bunch, with her snow-white paws, was the first to reach Ginger's feet.

Her purr was soft, like the hum of a distant motor, her sea-green eyes full of innocent curiosity as she peered up at Ginger.

Next was Gabriella, her fur an exquisite blend of sunset orange and pearl white that created unique swirls across her back. Her green eyes held a spark of mischievous intelligence that often led to escapades around the cabin.

Last to join was Geraldine, the runt of the litter, with her wild, untamed orange fur and wide-eyed curiosity. Geraldine, unlike her sisters, was a bit more timid, preferring the company of her siblings to adventures.

Ginger cradled them close, each one nestling into the warmth of her embrace, their soft fur tickling her skin. She brushed her fingers over the delicate patterns on their fur, committing each distinct marking to memory.

"I guess I'll have Myrtle come and get you," she choked out, her voice wavering. The three kittens, as though sensing her sadness, brushed their heads against her hand in a show of comfort. She'd left them plenty of food in their bowls and fresh litter boxes, making sure they would be comfortable until Myrtle arrived.

Kissing each kitten on the forehead, she

murmured her goodbyes then shut the cabin door and headed to the truck, resisting the urge to look back.

Ginger squeezed into Mason's truck. Her luggage was piled in the backseat. As they navigated the snow-covered roads, the truck's heater hummed, battling the biting cold outside. Despite the wintry conditions, a comforting sense of familiarity filled the cab as Mason guided them toward the Cozy Holly Inn.

"I know the Woodwards are happy to have you at the farm," Mason said.

"I know, but it just feels weird taking over the cottage. It's time for me to move out."

"You're welcome to stay with me and Dad. We have a bedroom on the first floor."

"I'm not kicking your dad out of his bedroom. Besides, you're kind of busy with Kristen, aren't you?" she teased.

Mason blushed. "I can make time for you."

Ginger laughed. "I like the inn. Their cooking is better than yours."

Arriving at the Cozy Holly Inn, Ginger was greeted by the familiar faces of the knitting club—Dorothy, Ida, Myrtle, and Mabel—all clustered around the fire, their needles clicking rhythmically.

Dorothy looked up, surprise etching lines onto her face when she saw Ginger's luggage. She put her knitting project—a bright fuchsia-and-orange hat that jutted out at strange angles—into her bag.

"Are you moving back to the inn?" Dorothy came over to stand next to her. "You know, you're welcome to stay with us as long as you want."

Ginger's heart tugged at the invite and the thought of staying on with the Woodwards. But if she couldn't save the trees, then she didn't deserve to stay. "Thank you, but I'm back on my feet again, so I figured I'd let Ethan have his place back."

Dorothy pulled her away from the bustling lobby and into the quiet sanctuary of the hall. "Is this about the trees?" she asked, the hallway's dimmed light softening the worry lines on her face. "Has your latest concoction worked?"

Ginger felt the familiar sting of disappointment. "Unfortunately, it hasn't. I did apply one last serum just before leaving the cabin, but..." She sighed. "I've told myself not to get my hopes up this time. I'm afraid if this one doesn't work, I'm out of ideas."

Dorothy clasped her hands together. "Well, there you go! This one might just be the miracle we need."

Ginger's heart fluttered at her optimism, but reality grounded her. "It might take some time to work, but unfortunately, well... I sort of told the mayor we'd have a tree for him to look at tonight."

Ginger could barely look Dorothy in the eye. Why in the world had she told the mayor they had a tree all picked out? She'd wanted to put him in his place because he was being a jerk, but she might have made things worse for the Woodwards.

Dorothy's eyes widened. "You did? And the trees might not be ready?"

Ginger shrugged. "I have no idea. The serum just went on an hour ago, so it will probably be too soon."

Dorothy's gaze drifted over Ginger's shoulder as the door opened, letting in a gust of frosty air. "Well, speak of the devil," she whispered.

"Mayor Thompson! So good to see you!" Ida's voice chimed from the living room. She hurried toward the mayor and offered to take his jacket and scarf.

He pulled an envelope from the inner pocket of his Canada Goose jacket. "The special permit for the parking for the New Year's Eve party came across my desk, and I figured I'd drop it off while I was in this part of town."

"Thank you so much." Ida tucked the envelope into her apron. "Won't you come in? I have fresh baked cookies and hot cocoa."

"Thank you, but I have to get to a meeting." He craned his neck toward the living room. "Ida, where's your Christmas tree?"

"Oh, I always wait until Christmas Eve. I like my trees fresh." Ida exchanged a glance with Dorothy. Apparently, Ida was in on the tree problem. She'd probably told the mayor she usually waited to throw him off the scent. Ginger liked her all the more for it.

Unfortunately, her glance at Dorothy made the mayor turn in their direction. He looked a bit taken aback, as if he hadn't realized they were there. Surprise flashed across his face, followed by a tinge of suspicion. Ginger's cheeks warmed, and she felt as if she'd been caught spying.

Acting like they were just coming down the hall, Ginger and Dorothy moved into the foyer, blending seamlessly into the conversation. As they engaged in small talk with the mayor, Ginger thought about her next move. Maybe she could persuade him to postpone his visit to see the tree tonight...

"I'm really looking forward to seeing the tree tonight, Ginger," he said, oblivious to the undercurrent of tension. "I've always admired how the Woodwards' tree lights up Pinecone Falls every Christmas Eve. Quite a sight."

His words hung in the air. Ginger glanced at Dorothy. How was she going to get out of this?

She pasted a smile on her face, not willing to let her anxiety show. "I hope it won't disappoint, Mayor

Thompson," she managed to say, trying to keep her voice steady.

"Indeed." The mayor's eyes narrowed, and then he turned toward the door. "Well, I must get to my next stop."

It was Ginger's last chance, and she acted before she even thought about it. As Mayor Thompson opened the door, she lurched forward, sending the bottom of her crutch right in front of him.

His right foot caught, and he lurched forward, falling out onto the front porch.

"I'm so sorry!" Ginger squeaked. "Me and my klutzy moves.... I hope you aren't hurt."

Dorothy ran over to the mayor, shooting Ginger a look of approval on her way over.

Scrambling to recover from her supposed accident, Ginger took in the scene around her. Dorothy and Ida had swooped in like a pair of overprotective hens, immediately fussing over the mayor, their voices a symphony of concern.

"Oh dear, Mayor Thompson!" Dorothy exclaimed, examining his ankle. "I think you might've sprained it."

"No, no." The mayor tried to dismiss their concerns, attempting to steady himself. "It's just a small stumble. I'm sure I'll be—"

"Nonsense!" Ida interrupted, her tone brooking no argument. "You should get it checked out at the emergency room. Better safe than sorry."

When he hesitated, Ida launched into a tale of her distant relative who had ignored a similar injury, ending up with a permanent limp and lifetime of regrets. The story, expertly woven with enough drama to rival any soap opera, had the desired effect. With a sigh of resignation, Mayor Thompson agreed to let Dorothy and Ida take him to the hospital.

As they ushered him out the door, Ida turned and winked at Ginger behind the mayor's back. Standing in the hallway, she watched the unlikely trio disappear into the snowy evening.

A spark of hope ignited in her chest. She'd managed to avert disaster—for now. But could she really save the day? Ginger allowed herself a moment to bask in that tiny glimmer of optimism. It wasn't much, but it was something.

CHAPTER 29

Ethan's truck crunched on the gravel as he pulled up to his cabin. He found Myrtle peering through the frosted glass of the front door.

"Myrtle?" Ethan's brow furrowed in confusion. Her presence, combined with her concerned look, made his stomach churn. Could something have happened to Ginger? Had she fallen again? "Is something wrong?"

"Oh, there you are, Ethan!" Myrtle exclaimed, turning to face him. "I was just coming by to see if you wanted me to take the kittens."

Ethan's brow furrowed in confusion. "Why would you think that?"

"Well"—Myrtle shrugged—"I saw Ginger at the

Cozy Holly Inn. I figured you might not want to take care of the kittens all by yourself."

Ethan felt like he'd been punched in the gut. "Ginger… She's at the inn?"

"Yes, she moved back," Myrtle said, her voice dropping to a sympathetic whisper. "She mentioned something about not wanting to be in your way. And I believe she was upset about the trees."

Ethan unlocked the door, and as he swung it open, the kittens scampered toward him, their tiny meows echoing around the empty cabin. He picked one up. Its soft fur was a comforting sensation against the sudden hollow feeling in his chest.

Myrtle watched as Ethan cuddled the kitten, a knowing smile playing on her lips. "Unless you want to keep them for a while…"

Ethan sighed. He'd grown attached and not just to the kittens. He didn't want to let them go. He didn't want to let Ginger go either. "Yes, I'll keep them."

Myrtle smiled. "Good! Then I'll leave you to it." Myrtle left, her departing footsteps crunching on the frost-laden path.

Ethan looked around at the now-too-quiet cabin. The tree they'd decorated stood in one corner, and the pine garland arranged along the windowsill spiced the air. He noticed a piece of paper sitting on the counter. It was a note in Ginger's neat handwriting.

I OWE you a thousand thanks and a million apologies. Your kindness and hospitality these past few days meant more to me than you can ever imagine, and I can only hope my thanks can make up for the burden I might have imposed.

I want you to know that I tried my best to help the trees. In my final effort, I prepared a serum which I believe could help, and Mason was kind enough to assist me in applying it to the trees. Unfortunately, it will need twenty-four hours to take effect.

And here comes my deepest regret. The mayor is due to visit this evening, far before the serum can do its job. I'm so sorry, Ethan. I wish I had come up with this solution sooner. The fear that I've potentially ruined everything is unbearable.

Again, thank you for letting me stay in the cabin even though I wasn't much help.

Yours sincerely,

Ginger

ETHAN CRUMPLED the note in his hand. The weight of Ginger's worries and his burgeoning feelings for her pressed on his chest. He glanced at the reminder buzzing on his phone—the mayor's meeting. But the urgency he felt was not for that. It was for Ginger.

Tossing his phone aside, he made a decision. He didn't care about the meeting or the mayor; he cared about Ginger. She was what mattered right now. With renewed determination, he grabbed the keys to his truck.

CHAPTER 30

Settled comfortably within the welcoming confines of the Cozy Holly Inn, Ginger rested her foot atop a cushiony footstool. A partially knitted scarf lay spread on her lap, each stitch meticulously crafted. Yet her focus kept straying from her task, her eyes continually drawn to the window. The bare winter vista outside beckoned to her, a poignant reminder of Ethan's cabin and the warmth she had left behind.

She shook her head, berating herself. Pinecone Falls was a world away from the bustling city she was accustomed to, a dream she had no business clinging to. She had made a promise to Mason to see out the holiday here. But when the festive glow faded, she would retreat to the familiarity of the cityscape.

The comforting click-clack of knitting needles filled the room as Ida, wise beyond her years, offered a sympathetic glance in Ginger's direction. With Dorothy at the ER with the mayor and the others having gone home, they shared a quiet solidarity.

The steady rhythm of their conversation hummed alongside the gentle clacking of knitting needles. Ida looked at Ginger, her eyes glinting with the wisdom of years. "Ginger, dear, not having a tree isn't the end of the world," she said, the lines on her face deepening with her warm smile.

Ginger gnawed on her lower lip, her brows furrowing as she responded, "Maybe not for us, Ida, but it might be for the Woodwards. This is their livelihood. They've built their lives around those trees."

Ida let out a soft chuckle, shaking her head. "The Woodwards are a resilient lot. They've been the backbone of this town for generations. Sure, the Christmas Eve tree ceremony is important, but do you truly believe that missing it once is going to unravel everything they've built?"

The question hung in the air, a challenge and reassurance mingled into one. Ida's calm conviction contrasted Ginger's fretful worry.

"You're being too hard on yourself," Ida advised gently, her experienced fingers navigating the yarn effortlessly. "You put your heart and soul into helping those trees. Who's to say your latest concoction won't work with a little time?"

"But time is a luxury we don't have." Ginger's gaze swiveled to the empty tree stand. "The mayor is itching to get his tree today, and there's none to give. What will this mean for the Woodwards?"

"Sounds a mite dramatic to me."

Am I being overly dramatic? Ginger wasn't sure, but Ida seemed to think so. Kringle sat beside Ida's rocking chair, his swishing tail narrowly avoiding the descending rocker with uncanny precision. Even he seemed to be looking at her as if she were making too much of the whole thing.

But watching Kringle reminded her of the three kittens. She missed them and hoped they would be okay. Myrtle would surely find good homes for them. With a soft sigh, she pondered, maybe a cat wouldn't be such a bad idea when she returned home.

"I'm sure Ethan doesn't think any less of you, dear." Ida's gaze drifted out the window, and Ginger followed it to see Ethan's truck pulling up in front.

"Looks like we have company. I'll get some cookies and cocoa." Ida jumped up from her chair, and Kringle followed her to the kitchen.

The front door swung open, and Ethan strode in,

his eyes finding Ginger immediately. His urgency stirred a flutter of self-consciousness in her. Had she left something at the cabin? Was there another problem with the trees?

"Ethan," she began, but he was already at her side, his breath labored from his rush.

"Ginger, there was no need for you to move out," he said, his voice carrying a raw honesty that had her heart hammering in her chest.

"I just thought, with me on crutches and messing things up with the mayor..."

He shook his head, taking her hand in his, his gaze intense. "I don't care about the mayor or the trees. They're not important. You are."

His confession hung in the air. That moment felt both fleeting and endless, a lifetime in the span of a heartbeat. She had just enough time to see the sincerity in his eyes. Ginger was stunned.

She opened her mouth to say something—she wasn't even sure what—but before she could get a word out, the front door crashed open. Dorothy stumbled in, her arms loaded with balsam pine branches, her entrance jolting them out of their moment, yet leaving behind the echo of a promise.

"Take a gander at these!" Dorothy barreled into the room, her arms loaded with fragrant balsam pine branches. With a whoosh of energy, she deposited the armful on Ginger's lap.

Ginger's eyes widened at the sight, her fingers tracing the branches gingerly. Ethan, who had been standing silently, watched with interest, his gaze softening at Ginger's evident excitement.

Dorothy, just noticing Ethan's presence, stammered a belated greeting. "Oh, hi, Ethan." Her gaze bounced between Ginger and Ethan. She frowned. "I didn't interrupt something, did I?"

Ginger dismissed the implied interruption with an excited wave of her hand, her attention fixed on the branches. "These look fantastic. Are all the trees like this now, Dorothy?"

Dorothy nodded. "I checked almost all of them at the farm."

Ethan leaned closer to get a better look, his shoulder brushing against Ginger's. She pointed out the telltale signs of healing. There was a remnant of the fungus, but a simple swipe of her finger cleaned it right off. The energy in the room shifted; a spark of hope ignited.

"See? It wipes away. We might just have a chance!" Ginger's voice echoed with excitement.

"A chance for what?" Ida came in with a tray of cookies and four mugs of cocoa.

"Ginger's serums worked on the trees!" Dorothy showed Ida excitedly.

"Well now, that is exciting." Ida handed mugs and cookies around.

"I knew you could do it!" Ethan looked adoringly at Ginger.

"Thanks, if only it wasn't too late." Ginger felt her hopeful feelings crushed. "The mayor is supposed to be looking at our trees tonight. We already missed our window, and now he's going to go to another tree farm."

Dorothy coughed, and a sly smile crept onto her face. "I don't think he's going to do that today, though. He might be tied up at the hospital until tomorrow. I happen to know one of the doctors, and they agreed that the mayor should stay in overnight."

"The hospital? Why is he in the hospital?" Ethan asked.

Ida's and Dorothy's eyes slid to Ginger, and she blushed. "He might have met with a little accident. You know how klutzy I am. My crutch slid out on the floor, and the poor mayor tripped on it."

Ethan laughed. "Well, I'd say we should be thankful for your klutziness. Besides, it's cute."

"Sounds like things might just work out after all."

Ida raised her mug. "To Christmas miracles and new beginnings."

Ginger clinked her mug with everyone else's. When she got to Ethan, their eyes met, and he repeated the words that were music to her ears. "To new beginnings."

CHAPTER 31

The town square was bursting with holiday cheer. Sculptures of reindeer, meticulously carved from ice, sparkled under the pale winter moon. A troupe of whimsical snowmen scattered about donned bright scarves and hats, and giant candy canes stood sentinel along the sidewalks, their red-and-white stripes stark against the blanket of snow.

Right in the middle stood a majestic twelve-foot balsam pine from Woodwards' Tree Farm.

"The tree is truly a sight to behold," Kristen sighed.

Ginger followed her gaze, and a sense of pride welled up in her. "It's one of your best," she responded, looking at Ethan, who was standing next to her.

His fingers laced with hers, sending a rush of warmth coursing through her despite the chill of the evening.

Julie chimed in, a playful glint in her eyes, "We were beginning to think the balsams were a myth! Holding out on us to build anticipation—quite the marketing strategy, eh?"

Their laughter echoed around them.

"We've almost sold out in the two days we've been offering them on the lot, so maybe we'll hold them back again next year." Ethan squeezed Ginger's hand.

"Only ten minutes to the lighting!" Dorothy said, fussily wrapping a flamboyant, hole-riddled scarf of pinks and purples around her neck. They all wore Dorothy's eccentric scarves—her unique knitting style was becoming a bit of a town sensation.

The soft jingle of bells alerted them to Nolan's arrival. He rode in on his sleigh, led by two horses, their manes swaying, their breaths fogging in the cold air. The bells attached to their harnesses jingled. Nolan pulled up beside them, a beaming smile on his face. "Who's up for a sleigh ride after the lighting?"

Ethan looked down at Ginger, and she nodded. "Sounds wonderful."

Across the expanse of the festive crowd, a familiar figure waved. "Hey there!" Myrtle's voice, cheerful and loud, carried over the thrum of the gathering. She made her way through the crowd. Her face lit up with a smile as she approached them.

"How are those kittens of yours doing?" she asked as she neared. "I bet they're getting into everything!"

A soft chuckle escaped from Ginger at the thought of the kittens' playful antics. "Oh, they sure are. But they're too cute to resist."

Ginger was still staying at the Cozy Holly Inn, but she spent most of her time at the cabin. Moving back in there was a thought she wasn't ready to entertain yet, but she was sure about one thing—Pinecone Falls was her future home. She'd already been looking at apartments with Kristen in town.

Mayor Thompson ascended the improvised stage beside the grand balsam pine, floodlights casting theatrical shadows around him. A tap on the microphone broke through the expectant hush, and the crackle echoed out across the winter-chilled crowd.

"Hasn't our dear mayor's disposition brightened tonight?" Myrtle teased, her eyes sparkling with a mischievous gleam.

Despite her reservations, Ginger found herself chuckling. "He does seem cheerful, albeit with a slight limp."

A knowing smirk graced Myrtle's features. "Sometimes, a fall serves as a good humbling experience."

A blanket of anticipation settled over the crowd as Mayor Thompson commenced the countdown. Voices melded together in a chorus of excitement, reverberating through the crisp night air.

"Three. Two. One!" they cried out as one, and with a triumphant flick, the mayor illuminated the tree. The crowd inhaled sharply as thousands of tiny white lights flickered to life, their radiance dancing off the gleaming ornaments and shimmering garland, bathing the town square in a magical, ethereal glow.

A murmur rippled through the bystanders, a voice softly exclaiming, "It's breathtaking." Julie's enthusiastic reply echoed in the stillness, "Nothing can rival the magic of Christmas Eve!"

As the applause swelled around them, Ethan turned Ginger toward him, his gaze locked on hers in the warm, mesmerizing glow. His voice was low yet steady, infused with sincerity. "Even amid this spectacle, Ginger, it's you who captivates me the most this Christmas Eve." And with those heartfelt words, he leaned in to kiss her, sealing the enchanting evening with a promise of many more to come.

ALSO BY MEREDITH SUMMERS

Lobster Bay Series:

Saving Sandcastles (Book 1)

Changing Tides (Book 2)

Making Waves (Book 3)

Shifting Sands (Book 4)

Seaside Bonds (Book 5)

Seaside Bookclub (Book 6)

Shell Cove Series:

Beachcomber Motel (Book 1)

Starfish Cottage (Book 2)

Saltwater Sweets (book 3)

Pinecone Falls Christmas Series:

Christmas at Cozy Holly Inn (Book 1)

Cozy Hometown Christmas (Book 2)

Meredith Summers / Annie Dobbs

Firefly Inn Series:

Another Chance (Book 1)

Another Wish (Book 2)

ABOUT THE AUTHOR

Meredith Summers writes cozy mysteries as USA Today Bestselling author Leighann Dobbs and crime fiction as L. A. Dobbs.

She spent her childhood summers in Ogunquit Maine and never forgot the soft soothing feeling of the beach. She hopes to share that feeling with you through her books which are all light, feel-good reads.

Join her newsletter for sneak peeks of the latest books and release day notifications:

https://lobsterbay1.gr8.com

This is a work of fiction.

None of it is real. All names, places, and events are products of the author's imagination. Any resemblance to real names, places, or events are purely coincidental, and should not be construed as being real.

GRUMPY COZY CHRISTMAS

Meredith Summers

http://www.meredithsummers.com

Created with Vellum